'Aidan?'

He looked startled.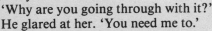

'Why?'

'Why what?'

'Why are you going through with it?'

He glared at her. 'You need me to.'

'But you don't *have* to,' she argued.

'Would you rather I didn't?'

'You don't have to. I can think of something else,' she went on frantically.

'What?' His voice held an emotion at last—scorn.

She didn't know. She hung her head. Her heart pounded painfully against her ribs. Why hadn't she just left things well enough alone? Why hadn't she quit while she was ahead?

'I . . . I could think of something,' she said finally.

Aidan snorted.

'You told me you didn't want to be married again,' she went on steadfastly, wishing she would shut up with every word she spoke. 'You said marriage was a trap. So why are you doing it?' *Say you love me*, she pleaded silently. *Tell me that's the reason.*

THE
MARRIAGE TRAP

BY

ANNE McALLISTER

MILLS & BOON LIMITED
ETON HOUSE   18-24 PARADISE ROAD
RICHMOND   SURREY   TW9 1SR

First published in Great Britain 1987
by Mills & Boon Limited

© Barbara Schenck 1987

Australian copyright 1987
Philippine copyright 1988
This edition 1988

ISBN 0 263 75891 5

Set in Times Roman 10 on 10¼ pt.
01-0288-59017 C

Printed and bound in Great Britain by
Collins, Glasgow

For Courtney

CHAPTER ONE

EVERYBODY said that once Courtney found Aidan Sawyer, her problems would be solved.

There wasn't a finer guide in the whole upper reaches of the Amazon jungle, they said. If anyone could help her find her missionary parents, he could, they said. If there was anyone she could depend on, it was Aidan Sawyer, they said.

Unfortunately 'they' seemed not to have told Aidan.

So when she finally tracked him down to the dank, overgrown backwater town of Boca Negra and actually found the finest guide to the upper reaches of the Amazon jungle sitting, bare-chested and grimy, amidst a dock full of mechanical clutter that had no doubt once been a boat engine, she had complete confidence that he would help her find her parents.

He said, 'No.'

Courtney stared, unable to believe she had heard him right. The din of market day, the cackle of chickens and the hawking of wares, must have befuddled her hearing. She stepped carefully into a coil of thick rope, edging part of it aside with her foot so that she could get closer.

'I beg your pardon.'

'No,' he enunciated very carefully. She heard traces of upper-class Boston in the word. The incongruity of it might have made her laugh if the word itself hadn't astonished and infuriated her. He *couldn't* say that!

'What do you mean, no?' She fished in her canvas bag and pulled out a crumpled, sweat-streaked business card. 'Aidan Sawyer, *guía e traductor*. Aidan Sawyer, guide and translator,' she read. 'That's you, isn't it?' She glowered through her owlish glasses at him. He was a great panther of a man, the quintessential jungle guide

despite the Harvard-educated voice. With his thick
unruly hair and hard-muscled body he was every inch
what she had expected him to be. Except willing.

She glanced around hopefully for another possible
Aidan Sawyer. The only person nearby was a tiny, dark,
wizened man in a shirt and trousers three sizes too large.
She didn't know whether to hope he was Aidan Sawyer
or not.

'It's me,' the panther agreed laconically. He squinted
up at her, his jade-green eyes unnerving. She didn't like
the way he was looking at her. It wasn't all that different
from the way a dozen other men had looked at her since
she had left Los Angeles five days ago, but it felt
different.

They had been assessing her, too—weighing the fact
that she was travelling alone and obviously wondering
whether they dared make a pass. But most had decided
that her cool, distant look and the way she used her large-
lensed glasses as a flirtation-proof barrier was reason
enough not to. She didn't think Aidan Sawyer was likely
to reach the same conclusion. He would probably
diagnose it as the myopia it was. The thought discon-
certed her.

'Well, then . . .?' she snapped irritably. 'You guide. It
says so right here.' She waved the card in front of his
nose.

He shrugged, the sheen of sweat on his mahogany
shoulders making the muscles glimmer. 'Nothing on the
card says I *have* to, though.'

Stymied, Courtney glared at him. Perspiration trickled
down her spine. She brushed a damp tendril of blonde
hair away from her face and wished she had thought to
get a haircut before she had left Los Angeles. The closest
thing to a hairdresser in Boca Negra was the old woman
in the market-place hacking up gourds with her machete.

The machete tempted her. She would have liked to
whack Aidan Sawyer with it. How dared he sit there and
simply decline to help her?

'Listen, Mr Sawyer,' she said, ignoring the small, dark man who was now winding up the large coil of rope that lay like an oily snake on the sun-bleached boards, 'I need to find my parents. I haven't heard from them in a year. And my uncle is threatening to—well, never mind what he's threatening to do.' There was no point in airing family disputes before a man who seemed totally uninterested anyway. 'Suffice it to say,' she went on, 'this is not some sort of lark I am undertaking, not some frivolous escapade to share with my high-society urban room-mates when I return.'

One sweat-darkened brow lifted. 'Got a lot of high-society room-mates, have you?' he drawled.

'I live alone,' she retorted sharply.

'Ah.' He seemed to consider that. 'That could be worth knowing.'

Courtney felt her cheeks burn. The old man coiling the rope snickered. If she had wondered how much of their conversation he understood, she now knew. Bristling, she snapped, '*You* will never have cause to be concerned about that.'

Aidan Sawyer's dark head bent over some bit of mechanical complexity. 'You're probably right.' He began to hum softly to himself, dismissing her.

Courtney glowered at him. He didn't notice.

'*Mr* Sawyer!'

The dark head lifted. He gave her a quizzical look.

'*Why* won't you take me?' She hated asking. But she couldn't argue with reasons she was unaware of, and she was definitely going to argue. She hadn't spent the last five days and the better part of her bank account in an effort to discover her parents' whereabouts, only to be turned back when she was within a hundred miles of them.

He didn't answer at once, not verbally anyway. His eyes raked her from the top of her straight, fair, shoulder-length hair to the tips of the painted pink toenails that peeped out of her Dr Scholl's sandals. They took in the off-white safari shirt that now, after several days' wear on plane, taxi, bus, and jeep, was closer to tan. They lingered far too long on her small breasts. They took in the wide leather belt and the baggy soft cotton slacks that had also once been white. They spoke volumes. But in case she didn't get the message, he spelled it out.

'Where'd you get the outfit? A yuppie safari store?'

Her cheeks flamed again, and not from the midday sun. 'As a matter of fact, yes, I did.'

He snorted. 'Figures.'

'I tried Army surplus first,' she told him sweetly. 'There's not a lot of gear made for people who are barely five foot four.'

Aidan grunted, as if he would rather not acknowledge that.

'So you're rejecting me on account of my clothes?' The moment she phrased it that way, she knew she had made a mistake. The old man's guffaw just confirmed it.

Grinning devilishly, Aidan shook his head. 'Sweetheart, I'm not rejecting *you* at all. I'm just not taking you into the jungle.'

Courtney took a deep breath, reminding herself that it was a hot day, that business was better conducted inside a semi-cool bar or café than in the midst of a sun-scorched dock. But she was reaching the limits of her patience. 'I'd like a reason, Mr Sawyer. A non-personal reason. If you can.'

For a moment she thought he would simply admit that he couldn't. Then he waved his hand over the dis-assembled engine parts. 'How about this?'

'Your engine, you mean?'

He nodded.

'How long will it take to fix it?'

He gave her a baleful look. 'As long as I want it to.'

She gritted her teeth. 'There's nothing wrong with it, then?'

He shrugged. 'A few new parts wouldn't hurt.'

'But you *could* get it going?'

Another shrug.

'I can wait.' Not for ever, but he didn't have to know that.

He sighed. 'It figures.'

'What's that supposed to mean?'

'It means, I guess, that I'll have to be blunt.'

Blunter than he already had been? Courtney couldn't quite imagine anything much blunter than the 'no' she had first received. 'By all means, Mr Sawyer, do speak your mind.'

He gave her a hard look. 'All right, I will.' Again she heard the hard New England clip in his voice. 'I won't take you because I'd have to be responsible for you. You'd shriek if a snake slithered across a limb in front of you. You'd howl when the rain ran down the back of your neck. You'd faint at the sight of a jaguar. And if you needed to use the gun, you'd probably shoot yourself in the foot. I guide experienced people—scientists, anthropologists, geologists. Not,' he added scathingly, 'schoolgirls whose hand I'd have to hold the whole damn way. I'm a guide, not a nanny, sweetheart. I don't guide people who need keepers. Like you.'

Well, he was blunt, she had to admit that. But it was all drivel. What did he know about her? 'Nonsense,' she told him flatly. 'I'm perfectly capable of taking care of myself. I am, after all, a grown woman.'

'In one way, anyhow,' he allowed, the way obvious from the once-over his eyes were giving her.

'Besides,' she went on doggedly, ignoring the heated suggestion in his eyes, 'I've been here before.'

'Oh yes? A Caribbean cruise with a fifty-mile day-trip up the Amazon, perhaps?' His voice dripped scorn.

'I was born and raised here.'

'In Boca Negra?' He was incredulous.

'In the jungle. I was born in Tuchanapi.' She named an Indian village about eighty miles away.

'Tuchanapi?' He frowned. Then a faraway gaze came into his eyes, as if he were remembering something. A moment later his gaze narrowed and he said, almost accusingly, 'You're the "white dolly"?'

It had been years since Courtney had heard that phrase. It brought back memories long forgotten. Stories about her mother's pregnancy, her father's insistence that if Indian children could be born there, so could his child; stories about how tiny she had been when she was born, and how the Indians in the village hadn't at first thought she was real, how they had persisted for several years in calling her 'White dolly' instead of her name.

For a moment she was shaken, and she suspected that he saw it in her face. Then she gave a wry smile of acknowledgement. 'I was.'

'Well, I'll be damned.' He cocked his head to one side and looked her over again, then grinned. 'You're still a dolly, too, by God.'

The old man cackled and nodded affirmatively, giving Courtney a toothless grin. 'She some dolly,' he chortled. 'You crazy not to take her, Saw-yer.'

Courtney, despite her annoyance, felt a momentary flicker of hope at having found an unexpected ally. But Aidan shook his head.

'Nope. Dollies are the last thing I need, João, and you damned well know it.'

'You like dollies,' João protested, still chuckling gleefully.

'Not like this one,' Aidan denied flatly.

'You don't need to talk about me as if I'm not even here!' Courtney snapped. 'I'm not in the least interested in being your "dolly". I only want to find my parents. And I will. With or without your help, Mr Sawyer!'

'Yeah?' He gave her an amused glance, as if she were a toddler throwing a tantrum. 'You and who else?'

'Me and whoever I can get, since you've declined.'

He frowned. 'You're out of your mind, lady. You pick some bandit to take you into the jungle and you'll never get out alive.'

'Well, it won't be any concern of yours, will it?' she asked him. 'Inasmuch as you've washed your hands of me.'

He let out a furious explosion of air. 'Lady, go home.'

'No.'

They glared at each other, hard green eyes battling equally stubborn blue ones. Courtney was glad she was the one standing. It was hard to be intimidating at her height. It would be impossible, she suspected, if he uncoiled his length. He must have been a shade over six feet, and he would tower over her.

He sighed and raked a hand through his thick dark hair. It was curling in the humid air, and it wanted cutting even more than hers did. 'Look, Miss...Miss...' He stopped suddenly, obviously realising for the first time that he didn't even know her name.

'Miss Perkins,' she informed him crisply. 'Mary Courtney Perkins.'

'Mary Courtney? Sounds like a nun.' He looked at her suspiciously. 'You're not, are you?'

'No.'

'A schoolteacher,' he guessed.

She sighed. 'I write children's books.'

'Children's books? Like Goldilocks and Winnie the Pooh? You write about bunnies and stuff?' He tilted back his head and laughed, a strong rough masculine laugh.

'That amuses you, Mr Sawyer?'

'It puts my mind at ease,' he told her. 'Now I know I was right in refusing you. Listen, Miss Mary Courtney Perkins, you may have been born out here——' he waved a hand towards the dark green forest surrounding them '—and you may have fond memories of a Garden of Eden childhood where Mommy and Daddy protected their little girl from danger, but this is not Kipling's "altogether uninhabited interior". This is the real live jungle we're talking about. And people who protect *big* girls aren't thick on the ground.'

Courtney rested a hand on her hip. 'Any minute now I expect you'll remind me that it's a "bunny eat bunny" world out there.'

He stared at her, a tiny smile playing at the corners of his mouth. 'You wouldn't listen if I did.'

'Absolutely correct.'

He shook his head. 'You'll just go out and hire yourself some bandit or rapist or murderer, and set off into the jungle with him.' He tossed the engine part he had been cleaning on to the dock and got to his feet.

'If you insist,' Courtney said more blithely than she felt. She had been right. Vertical he was more than imposing. Downright menacing summed it up.

'It's not *me* who's insisting, sweetheart,' he told her. He took the end of the rope from João and ambled away down the dock towards the long narrow boat tied up at the end.

'Go on home. You're out of your element here,' he tossed back at her.

'That remains to be seen.'

He glanced over his shoulder, beginning to wrap the rope in a wide loop around his elbow and forearm. 'You need a demonstration?'

She stuck her chin out. 'You're damned right I do.'

A slow grin lit his face. 'You asked for it, sweetheart.' And he gave a quick twist of the rope. Immediately she felt the other end tighten around her ankle. One swift yank and he had swept her off her feet. The next thing she knew muddy river water was closing over her head.

Spluttering, gasping, she struggled to the surface. 'Why, you——!' Water streamed down her face as she floundered towards the dock, blinking and shaking her head. A hand reached down to pull her out. Shaking the hair out of her eyes, she looked up at Aidan's grinning face.

'Never stand in a rope coil, Miss Perkins,' he drawled in his Boston-twang voice. 'Lesson number one.' He leaned over further, his lean brown hand outstretched. For a split second she considered not taking it. Then she thought, why not? and took a firm grip.

A second later Aidan Sawyer was thrashing in the water beside her.

'God Almighty!' he roared breaking the surface.

'Never mess with a lady who writes about bunnies and stuff, Mr Sawyer,' she said and hoisted herself soggily up on to the dock. 'Lesson number two.'

As she dripped her way up the steps to the road, she heard João chuckling, 'I guess she show you.'

What she had shown him, Courtney thought gloomily once she was in her hotel room stripping off her sopping clothes, was that he had been right to refuse her.

No man in his right mind would trek off into the jungle with a woman who dunked him for spite. But he had dunked her first! she remembered with renewed fury. To teach her a lesson! He'd got one, too, though. So now they were even. Perhaps, she tried encouraging herself as she dragged a brush through her still wet hair, he would respect her daring and change his mind.

Unfortunately even she wasn't that big an optimist.

And she was less so half an hour later when she went back out into the lobby-cum-café of the town's only hotel, a dreary damp one-storey wooden building that had definitely seen better days, and asked Consuelo, the smiling, round-faced woman who checked people in, waited on tables, cleaned rooms and did everything else that needed doing, if she knew the way to Aidan Sawyer's heart.

'Heart? You want his heart?' The older woman laughed. 'I thought you want a guide.'

'It's just an expression,' Courtney assured her. 'I do want a guide. But he wasn't too eager——' which was putting it mildly '—so I need to do a bit of persuading.'

Consuelo clicked her tongue. 'Persuade that one? Money maybe. He needs a new motor for his boat. Or, you don't got money, there are other things he might like.' She gave a creditable imitation of Aidan cataloguing Courtney's feminine charms.

'Not that,' Courtney said quickly.

Consuelo shrugged. 'Then money, I guess.'

Courtney had some, but probably not enough to sway Aidan Sawyer when he seemed already to have made up his mind against her. She sighed and leaned against the counter, watching as Consuelo folded the almost threadbare towels. Surely there must be some way under the man's guard. But she couldn't think what. Maybe if she had a bit of time, she could figure it out.

But time was something she had very little of, she realised moments later when she heard, 'Mama! Mama! Guess what! We got guests coming!'

Consuelo's son, Aurelio, the ten-year-old charmer who had carried Courtney's duffel bag from the bus while giving her a Chamber of Commerce spiel about the highlights of Boca Negra, shot in the door, a large canvas bag in each hand.

'Scientists! Writers! Everybody!' He made it sound like a full-scale invasion.

By Boca Negra standards, Courtney supposed it was, when shortly afterwards a group of four dusty men appeared.

'Rooms for the night?' the tallest one asked Consuelo.

She nodded happily, handing out keys, giving rapid-fire directions to Aurelio who lugged their bags down the hall to the rooms she indicated.

'You be here long?' she asked while the man signed the ledger.

'Only overnight if we can manage it. We're doing an ecological study of one of the tributaries.' He glanced up. 'We need a good guide.'

'Aidan Sawyer,' Aurelio said importantly. 'He's the best.'

Courtney glared at him.

'Think he's available?' the man asked.

Consuelo shrugged her ample shoulders. 'Don't know. You can ask him. He's down at the dock.'

'Which tributary?' Courtney asked suddenly. If the men were only going in the same direction as she was . . .

They weren't. 'How long will you be gone?' she asked him.

'A month, I reckon.'

'A *month*?' If they took Aidan Sawyer away for a month, chances were she would never get to her parents in time. 'Aren't there some other guides, Consuelo?' she asked a bit desperately when the man left.

'Raimundo Pereira. But I would not like to see you go with him.'

'Why not?'

Consuelo weighed her words before answering. 'If you say no to Aidan Sawyer, I think he will respect that. He does not want to get, how do you say, "involved" with a woman. He does not want to be...' She paused, groping for the word in English.

'Responsible,' Courtney guessed grimly.

Consuelo nodded at once. 'Yes. That's it. He would feel "responsible". Raimundo, he won't care.'

Swell. Raimundo was probably the bandit-rapist-murderer Aidan had in mind.

'I didn't mean for me,' she said quickly. 'I meant for the men. Surely if *they* said no...'

Consuelo giggled. 'Raimundo would not bother them. But he gets drunk a lot. Aidan don't. They will want Aidan.'

Courtney thought they would, too. And Aidan would want them.

'I'm going out for a while,' she told Consuelo. 'I need to think.'

She considered all the available alternatives. There weren't many. She could, of course, turn back. But if the law firm doling out the trust that her grandfather had left to both her father and Uncle Leander wasn't handed concrete evidence within six weeks that her father was still alive, Leander was going to be able to break the trust that would care for her parents in their old age. And while her parents never seemed to care about that, Courtney did.

Endicott 'Chippy' Perkins and his wife, Marguerite, were in many ways like children. They embodied the best of Christian charity, and they never gave a thought to tomorrow. They were lilies of the field, confident that God's bounty would be there for them.

It would be. But only if, while they didn't worry about the future, Courtney did. She knew that, however much they might like to stay in the jungle for ever, they wouldn't be able to. Her father's arthritis had been worse a year ago, when she had last got a letter from them. He was having trouble getting around. Her mother's eyesight wasn't good. She knew the time would come when they would have to retire from their missionary activities. And she also knew they fully expected to come back to the States and live on the inheritance that Endicott's father had left in trust for him and his brother.

If Leander didn't get his hands on it first.

Courtney scowled, remembering that Leander had already put his lawyers to work on it. She had protested. But Leander had merely shrugged. 'I haven't heard from Chippy in years,' he reminded her.

It wasn't surprising. Her parents thought in terms of whoever was in front of them and whoever needed their help right then. Leander, being well heeled and in Beverly Hills to boot, was undoubtedly at the bottom of their list. But Courtney had heard from her parents, and she said so.

'That's nice.' Leander had steepled his fingers and peered over the top of them at her like a vulture contemplating a meal. 'But Chippy has to check in with the firm once a year. He hasn't.'

Her father would never remember such a thing. Her parents scarcely seemed even to remember her. It had been over a year since her mother's last letter.

'Maybe they're missing,' Leander suggested.

'I don't think so,' Courtney replied stiffly.

'Or maybe they've been eaten.' He was warming to the idea.

'Uncle Leander!'

'Just kidding.' He smiled, but it was a crafty smile, and she knew quite well he probably wouldn't have cared if they had been or not. Money was the only thing that interested Leander.

'I'll find them,' Courtney promised.

'Do that,' her uncle said, but he didn't sound as if he hoped she would succeed.

She would though, she vowed. Her parents had spent their lives in service of others. It was time someone looked out for them.

And the someone was going to be her.

It wasn't an entirely unselfish motive that drove her, she acknowledged. She knew only too well that if she didn't save their inheritance and their independence, someday they would move in with her. And the simple knowledge that if they gained a toehold in her life, they would pick out a husband for her, rearrange her furniture, and name her children, was enough incentive to send her to South America at once.

It was not just their future she was saving, but her own.

But that meant getting Aidan Sawyer to guide her. Back to square one.

'Bunnies and stuff,' she muttered wryly. If he only knew! She wrote children's adventure fiction and fantasies, and while she might not have tangled with every sort of beast in her books, she had kayaked every river, climbed every mountain, and hiked every trail that her protagonists had. She was probably in better shape than he was, did he but know it.

But he didn't. Aidan Sawyer thought she was a nambypamby who would require an infinite amount of coddling. And Leander thought he would be able to bust the trust without her stopping him. Neither of them knew that for obvious reasons her father had nicknamed her 'Mule'.

Well, they would learn. Leander, hopefully, within a month or so; Aidan Sawyer, far sooner than that.

'They are going in the morning,' Consuelo told her that evening as she washed the dishes in the back of the café.

'With Aidan?'

'Yes.' Consuelo gave her a sympathetic glance.

'He got his engine fixed, did he?'

'Must have. They leave at dawn.'

'Dawn? When's dawn?'

Consuelo's eyes narrowed. 'Just past five this time of year. You're not thinking of stowing away, are you?'

'Me?' Courtney laughed. 'Not on your life. They're going in the wrong direction, remember? The last thing anyone knew of my folks they were east of here.'

Aurelio came in just then, his pet sloth, Slow Hand, casually draped over his shoulder. 'I take you,' he offered.

Consuelo shuddered. 'You will not.'

Aurelio's face fell.

'Maybe when you're older,' Courtney consoled him.

'Better me than Raimundo,' Aurelio said to his mother.

She grunted, then reached over and patted Courtney on the arm with a soapy hand. 'Maybe you not meant to go.'

Courtney shook her head. 'No. I'm going all right.'

'But——'

She wrapped her fingers over Consuelo's dark hand. 'Don't worry about me. I'll work something out.'

CHAPTER TWO

'NANCY DREW, where are you when I need you?' Courtney muttered as she surreptitiously lifted the holey screen off the hotel room window and prepared to drop to the ground below.

She had always taken the adventures of the teenaged fictional detective with more than a grain of salt, skimming rather than reading them with the thoroughness they had obviously deserved. If she had paid attention, she would not be having such a difficult time sneaking around now.

Thank heavens it was only a one-storey building. If it hadn't been, her parents might have done without their inheritance. But the ground was soft when she landed, and she looked around, breathing a sigh of relief.

Why she felt relief, she had no idea. The hard part hadn't even started yet. Wiping damp palms on the sides of her trousers, she loped along quietly in the shadows of the buldings down towards the dock.

She ought to have asked Consuelo where Aidan Sawyer lived. As it was, he might pop up at any second. But a careful look around reassured her. No one in the entire town seemed to be moving. Even the birds were quiet. Only an occasional loud shriek rent the air.

Ducking down just in case someone did happen to be looking, she crept quietly out on to the dock. Aidan Sawyer's boat was still tied up at the end, its engine now firmly in place.

Courtney didn't know a lot about engines. If she had been asked to fix one, she would have been quite sure she couldn't do it. But breaking one, at least temporarily, didn't seem beyond her capabilities. All she had to do, she figured, was remove something vital.

If she had stopped to think, she wouldn't have been doing it at all. It was against every moral precept she had ever met. But so was what Leander was trying to do to her parents. And if she had to justify it, she supposed she would mutter something about the lesser of two wrongs.

Fortunately no one was asking for a justification.

She knelt down on the dock next to the boat, grabbed the stern which swayed a few feet away, and drew it up against the split-tyre buffer that lined the boards of the dock. Then she eased herself over into the boat and pulled the engine up out of the water.

A screwdriver wouldn't have been amiss. But while she carried a lot of things in her bag, she didn't have one of those. And Aidan Sawyer hadn't left his tools lying around. She searched her pockets for a dime, and, finding one, she set to work.

Removing the engine casing took longer than she liked. Her fingers fumbled, she swore under her breath. The boat bobbed, making her hand slip time and time again. But at last she had it off.

A sudden scuffling and noise from the street above made her freeze, then crouch as low as she could. The voices were loud and slurred. Peeping up carefully, she caught sight of two men weaving their way towards the dock. She held her breath, praying that one of them wasn't Sawyer.

Her prayers were answered. The men were both too short, and neither of them spoke like a Harvard graduate. They weaved off at last and went into the side door of the general store that she had passed on the way down. Perhaps one of them was the proprietor. She hoped so. That meant he wouldn't be coming back out again. She didn't need any more interruptions. It was already past two. If Aidan Sawyer and his entourage thought they were going to leave at dawn, they would be down at the boat by four to load it. Taking a quick look over her shoulder, she set back to work.

In the end it wasn't too difficult. She simply removed a screw here and a screw there, and for good measure she took a rubber belt and something that she suspected would whirr round and round once you got the engine started. If it worked with all those parts gone, she guessed divine providence was telling her not to meddle in Uncle Leander's affairs.

Then she and her dime set to work replacing the engine casing. That, unfortunately, took even longer than it had to take it off.

It was five minutes past three when she climbed back into her window at the hotel. She narrowly missed running into one of the scientists who was just coming out on to the porch, obviously getting ready for an early start.

'Whew.' She sank on to her bed in relief, and was horrified to hear a resounding clank.

'Damn!' She got up again and very carefully buried her noisy treasures beneath her mattress. Then she undressed and slid silently under the sheet, rolling on to her side and waiting for the sounds of morning.

In fact, she missed them. The sleepless night that had followed two miserable days on the bus, followed by her pre-dawn assault on Aidan's boat, had finished her off. She was asleep before the scientists left. And she was still sleeping when Aurelio knocked on her door at ten o'clock in the morning.

'I bring you some chocolate, all right?' Brown eyes and a wide grin took in her befuddled expression. 'You sleep a long time.'

Courtney blinked, lifting herself on one elbow. 'Huh? Oh, er, yes, I guess I did.' She glanced at her watch. Ten o'clock! Merciful heavens! 'D...did the, uh, expedition leave, then?'

'The scientists, you mean?'

She nodded, taking the cup of steaming chocolate from him and sipping it carefully.

'Not yet,' Aurelio said cheerfully. 'They got a problem with the boat.'

Courtney tried to look amazed. 'Oh?'

'It don't work again. Aidan, he is mad. He says that rat Raimundo sabotage it.'

'Does he?' Better and better. She allowed herself another sip and followed it with a smile.

Aurelio put a plate of fried bread on the rickety table beside her bed. '*Sim*. He thinks Raimundo do it to get the job.'

'*Did* Raimundo get the job?'

'If Aidan don't get the boat fixed by noon. And,' he added with a grin, 'if the men get Raimundo sobered up by then.'

'May the Lord help them in their noble efforts,' Courtney intoned.

'What?'

'I hope they do,' she translated for him.

'Aidan don't,' Aurelio said frankly. 'He says he madder than spitting nickels.' He looked at Courtney to confirm whether he had got the colloquialism right or not.

'I'll bet he is,' she murmured. She gave Aurelio a smile. 'Thanks for the chocolate.'

'*De nada.*' He started to turn when he frowned suddenly, looking down at the floor. 'What's that?'

Courtney looked over the side of the bed to see him bend down and pick up one of the larger screws that had been part of her booty. 'I—uh, I can't imagine.'

Aurelio squatted down, scowling at the bed frame. 'Too big for here.' He considered the worn, slightly rusty screw in his hand, then he tipped his head up and looked wide-eyed at Courtney. 'Don't look like a bed-frame screw.'

'It don't? I mean, it doesn't?'

He stood up and grinned, tossing the screw up in the air and catching it. She held her breath. Then he stretched out his hand and gave it to her. 'I never tell,' he said.

* * *

'I suppose Aurelio tell you,' Consuelo said to Courtney half an hour later, scarcely glancing up from the huge stewpot into which she was flinging all manner of chopped vegetables.

'About the expedition, you mean?'

'*Sim.*' She shook her head. 'That Raimundo!'

Courtney felt a brief pang of guilt at having Raimundo blamed by all for her own deviousness. But moments later when she saw the scruffy man, now mostly sober and chattering away a mile a minute as he walked with two of the scientists towards the dock, she felt better.

For one thing, he didn't look any better than Aidan Sawyer had led her to believe he was, and she knew she didn't want to go out in the jungle with him. For another, she thought the scientists might handle him admirably. They would daunt him instead of the other way around. And he definitely looked as if he could use the money.

Aidan Sawyer, she noted as she glanced out into the café, looked somewhere between furious and grim. She was glad it was Raimundo he was angry with, not her.

'What a pity,' she said brightly. 'Want me to help you with the vegetables?'

Consuelo gave her a shrewd look. 'The better for you I would think.'

Courtney knew better than to pretend she had no idea what Consuelo was getting at. 'Only if he changes his mind.'

Consuelo grunted. She handed Courtney a knife and nodded at the heap of vegetables on the table. They worked in silence. After the spicy meat and vegetable *feijoado* was simmering on the stove, Courtney helped Consuelo make up beds, sweep floors and hang washing. Nothing was said about her dogging Consuelo's footsteps; nothing was said about the way she vanished when one of the scientists came back to announce that they were leaving with Raimundo; nothing was said about the way she smiled with relief when Raimundo's boat, laden so heavily that it barely had three inches of freeboard, disappeared upstream.

Nothing was said at all until that afternoon when Aurelio came back into the hotel, Slow Hand draped over his shoulder again. 'You going now?' he asked Courtney.

'Going where?' his mother wanted to know.

'No, I——'

'Going to see if Aidan take her.' Aurelio had no qualms about discussing it apparently, now that the scientists had gone. 'She is very tricky, Mama.'

'I thought you weren't going to tell.' Courtney gave him a dark look.

Consuelo gave her an assessing one. 'Is that so?'

'Very tricky.' Aurelio winked. He reached up and scratched the sloth's back.

'I don't think I will just yet,' Courtney said. 'I have some things that need doing in my room.' And so saying she vanished down the hallway. It wouldn't do, no matter what Aurelio thought, to pop out the moment Raimundo had disappeared upstream. Discretion was the better part of valour, after all.

It was also the better part of staying on Aidan Sawyer's good side. Presuming, of course, that he had one. So she kept to the background, wondering, as she did so, how she was going to be able to contrive to get the engine parts back to him.

It wouldn't do simply to show up with them and claim to have found them. She might have been able to outwit him once, but she wasn't going to try to make a habit of it.

As it happened, though, she didn't have to try. Aurelio did it for her.

'I jus' tol' him I find them when I'm taking out the trash,' Aurelio explained that evening when he poked his head in her door and gave her a thumbs-up sign. 'So tomorrow you can maybe ask him again?' His grin was conspiratorial.

Courtney gave him a hug. 'You're a pal.'

But she still felt a bit guilty the next morning when she walked down towards the dock. Only the knowledge that she had done it for a higher good allowed her even to face Aidan Sawyer again.

He was sitting on the end of the dock, staring upriver, his elbows resting on his knees, his chin in his palm. He did not look happy. She walked the length of the dock, debating whether she should make a noise and warn him or whether she should be quiet until she got to him. As it happened, her shadow fell across him, and he glanced over his shoulder. His expression was not welcoming.

'You again?'

She gave him a bright smile. 'I see you got your engine fixed.'

He scowled. 'Which time?'

'The last time I saw you it was all over the dock.'

'Surely you couldn't have failed to hear about the time *after* that one.' He stood up slowly, towering over her. She glanced down to make sure she didn't happen to be standing in a rope coil again. He saw where her eyes flickered and a grin was tugging at the corner of his mouth.

'Well, I did hear a rumour or two,' she allowed.

'I'll bet you did.' He stuffed his hands into the pockets of his shorts and looked her up and down again. Two of the scientists had given her that same sort of appraising look, and Courtney hadn't turned a hair. But whenever Aidan Sawyer looked at her, she turned to flame.

'So, are you interested in a job?' she asked him with as much nonchalance as she could muster.

'I thought we'd been over all that.'

'I thought you might've changed your mind.'

He looked at her narrowly. 'And why would I do that?'

She shrugged lightly. 'Finances, perhaps. I mean, since you didn't get the expedition job... And you did say something about wanting a "few new parts" for the engine. Besides,' she added, 'I thought you'd rather have any job than none at all.'

'You did, did you?' His green eyes got even narrower. He looked at her long and hard, then his eyes moved slowly from her to his engine. It wasn't hard to guess what he was thinking.

'Nice day, isn't it?' she commented inanely.

He frowned at her. 'Is it? A nice day for setting someone up, you mean?'

'I don't know what you're talking about.' She crossed her fingers behind her back.

'Odd how it was Aurelio who found those engine parts. I wouldn't have guessed Raimundo would hide them near his place.'

'Well, er, you never know, do you?'

'No,' he said with a grim smile. 'You never do.' He let out a long breath with an expletive in it somewhere. Then he said, 'I am beginning to believe it's possible that you're not as innocent as you look.'

She didn't know whether to confirm or deny that. If ever there was a trick question...

But she didn't have to. He went right on. 'You're beginning to strike me as a damned determined lady, Miss Mary Courtney Perkins.'

She drew herself up to her full five foot four inches. 'I told you that.'

'And I wouldn't be surprised then if I never did get another commission as long as I keep refusing you.'

She coloured fiercely. 'Well, I don't know how you can say that. I just——'

He glowered at her. 'Don't tell me what you just. I don't think I want to know. If I take you, you'd better keep up that determination, you understand?'

A shaft of hope touched her heart. 'I understand. Oh, absolutely.'

'No bellyaching. No whining. No begging to come back. You take care of yourself.'

'Of course.'

'We find your parents. You do whatever it is you came for. We come back. All straightforward. Understood?'

'Understood.'

'And you'll leave my boat alone.'

She tried to look offended. He wasn't impressed.

'I will most assuredly leave your boat alone, Mr Sawyer. Does this mean I've hired you?'

He scowled. 'You've hired me.' He turned and hopped lightly down into the boat, beginning to pull the tarp off something in the bow.

'Thank you.'

'I won't say you're welcome, Miss Perkins. And I doubt you'll be thanking me before we're through. Just remember, this is what you want.'

'It is,' she said more stoutly than she felt.

'Be ready at dawn. I'm sure you won't have any trouble getting up that early.'

She shook her head. 'No, I'm quite used to it.'

He gave her a black look. 'I'll bet.'

Guiltily she turned and scurried back up the dock. But she couldn't contain the spurt of satisfaction that bubbled up within her, not even when the last words she heard him say to João were, 'I think she has more in common with Lucrezia Borgia than Little Bo-Peep.'

CHAPTER THREE

'BE careful what you pray for, since you will surely get it,' her father always used to say. But Courtney, never having got the pony or the skates at Christmas, nor having ever been asked by Troy Williams to her high-school prom, nor having had her first book accepted by the first publisher to look at it, had never given that particular theological advice the respect it deserved.

Until now.

But as she piled her gear into Aidan Sawyer's boat and watched him stow it away, she began to develop that respect. For if she had boxed Aidan into a corner and coerced him into taking her along, thereby getting what she wanted, she had got something else besides—she had got Aidan Sawyer.

For at least two weeks, she and Aidan Sawyer would be a team. Just the two of them. Together. In a boat only twice as long as a bathtub and just about as wide.

Two weeks with a man like Aidan Sawyer was a daunting prospect.

If he had been the lawyer she had been dating at home, she wouldn't have given it another thought. She and Clarke Battersby had sailed to Catalina and hadn't got in each other's way or on each other's nerves once. They had never made love either because they respected each other too much.

Somehow Courtney couldn't see Aidan having that much respect.

He and Clarke were at opposite ends of the spectrum of male behaviour. Clarke was all polish, control and clearly defined goals. Aidan, from what she could see—upper-class Boston accent notwithstanding—was rough, ready and probably had no idea of where his next meal was coming from. Nor did he seem to care. Chances were he preferred it that way. Another 'lily of the field'? Hardly. A clump of crabgrass was more like it.

'That it?' Aidan finished stowing her gear in the boat and turned to give her the full benefit of his haunting green eyes.

'That's it.' Courtney wished it had been the heat that was making her feel oddly breathless. But she was fairly sure it wasn't. She tried to remember that he was the employee, she was the employer, and that she had coerced him into this.

He slung his own duffel bag into the back of the boat and carefully set a gleaming rifle down beside it. The sight of it made Courtney shudder, but she was careful not to comment. She didn't have to. He saw her expression and treated her to a disdainful one of his own. 'Tool of the trade, Bo-Peep,' he told her. 'You ready?'

'Yes.'

'Let's go, then.'

She was prepared to decline if he offered her his hand to help her into the boat. He didn't. He simply jerked his head towards the bow. 'You sit there.'

'Right.' She stepped gamely in and settled herself on the narrow plank seat. Turning, she gave him what she hoped was an eager smile. 'All set.'

He grunted and yanked the starter rope on the small engine. Courtney held her breath, but apparently he had been able to get all those assorted screws and other gizmos back on properly, for the engine roared to life. The three onlookers on the dock cheered.

'Be careful,' Consuelo admonished, waving her dish towel.

'Have fun,' Aurelio called. *'Boa viagem.'*

'Não faze nada que eu não faría,' João called to Aidan.

'Don't do anything I wouldn't do?' Courtney translated. She glanced over her shoulder at Aidan.

'Fat chance,' he said.

They travelled quickly and silently downriver until the sun was high in the sky. The river itself broadened as they moved south-east, and the canopy of the jungle receded far enough to allow the midday sun to beat down on them mercilessly for a brief time. Then the clouds built up and it rained. Courtney remembered the pattern well. She had lived in this jungle for twelve years, until her parents had deemed her old enough to send her away to school. And one of the things she remembered best was that she had never been quite dry the whole time. She had thought it was a normal, if annoying, way to live until the first year she spent in California at a girls' school where she had learned that dampness was not a way of life.

The first time the skies opened up, they were just heading into rough water where the river narrowed and flowed faster. Courtney clamped her hat down tightly on her head, then gripped the gunwales of the boat to keep herself from being thrown in as they went shooting forward. The boat pitched and bucked. Gritting her teeth, she hung on for dear life. Then Aidan cut the boat across the rapids skilfully, avoiding the surge of the main channel, and all at once they were in a quiet eddy, the danger past. Courtney breathed again. She sighed and glanced back at Aidan.

He grinned at her. It was a wicked grin, one that dared her to complain as the water that coursed down her cheeks and drenched her clothes, that dared her to utter one word about the danger they had just passed—the danger she had insisted he bring her into.

Not in a million years, she thought stubbornly.

'Suit you, duckie?' he shouted over the torrents of rain that thundered down around them.

'To a T,' she shouted back and turned away from him.

The next time the skies opened, they were in a wider channel, and Aidan aimed their boat towards a log lying half in the river and cut the engine. Courtney looked back at him, frowning. 'What's wrong?'

'Nothing. I want a swim.'

'A swim?'

'Sure. Why not? We're soaking wet anyway.' He didn't wait for a reply. As he spoke, he was unbuttoning his shirt and casting it aside. Then he stripped off his trousers. She swallowed hard at the sight of hard-muscled bare thighs. He lifted his eyebrows at her, smirking. 'Enjoying the view?'

Steam was probably rising from her cheeks where the rain hit them. She jerked her gaze away abruptly and didn't even see him dive into the water. She only felt the lurch of the boat. Turning back, she saw a pair of white briefs cast on top of the trousers he had discarded, and she felt a brief pang of regret that she hadn't waited a few moments longer before she had averted her eyes. Then, embarrassed at the direction of her thoughts, she tried to remember the purpose of her trip. It wasn't easy, especially once he surfaced several yards away, shook the hair out of his eyes and grinned at her.

'Come on in. The water's fine.'

'No thanks.'

The grin turned into a smirk again. 'Don't tell me you're too shy.'

'I won't, then,' she said stiffly. But if the truth were known, she was. Swimming naked with someone like Clarke wouldn't have even fazed her, and she knew it. Not, of course, that Clarke would ever have suggested such a thing. But with Aidan Sawyer—forget it! He was too intimidatingly masculine!

Still, she wished she dared. She felt as if she were being steamed alive while the rain came down. When it stopped things got even worse. Her clothes stuck to her. Her glasses steamed up. Her hair clung to her head. If she had had a pair of scissors handy, she would have hacked it off then and there. She wished they could get moving again. But that meant Aiden clambering naked out of the water...and that meant seeing him... Whoa, sweetie, she reminded herself. You don't have to watch.

But, heavens, she was tempted. The way he cut through the water like a seal made her all too aware of his natural male grace. And watching him arch and dive under, presenting her with a flash of muscular buttocks, tantalised her. She was breathing as if she had run a mile when he finally swam over to the boat and hoisted himself over the side.

She averted her face, but not before she had seen all of him. He would have put Clarke Battersby to shame. Ducking her head, she pretended great interest in the flotsam and jetsam slipping down the river past them.

'Pass me a towel,' Aidan commanded.

She did, lifting her eyes only as far as his knees. The view of dark hairs plastered against his firm legs made her want to raise her head higher. Stubbornly, she didn't.

Aidan sighed as he rubbed his body. 'You're crazy,' he said conversationally. 'You ought to swim.'

Courtney allowed herself only a grunt in response. She saw him step into his briefs, then pull on his trousers, and heard him zip them up. At last she lifted her eyes. He was looking down at her with amusement on his face.

'I suppose you think if you're naked, I'll ravish you.'

She didn't answer that at all.

'I won't,' he said. 'Not yet, anyway.' And then, slipping on his shirt, he said, 'Hand me a banana, will you?' as if his earlier words had been no more than a figment of her imagination.

Flustered, she handed him one, taking one herself. He took his without thanking her, peeled it and bit into it, disregarding the rain that had started up again and sluiced down his face. He was too busy staring at her, an undecipherable expression on his face.

Finally he said, 'You should have gone swimming. It wouldn't have made any difference.' A grin quirked the corner of his mouth.

Courtney frowned, squinting at him, then took her glasses off and tried to dry them on her shirt-tails so that she could see what he was looking at so earnestly. One glance downwards was all it took. He was looking at her!

He was staring right through her translucent safari shirt which had obviously not been designed to be worn in tropical rainstorms. Not in mixed company anyway. It was no secret now that she wasn't wearing a bra today. The dusky aureoles of her breasts were only too visible. No wonder Aidan was staring. She blushed and ducked her head, rooting around in another of the packs for a vinyl poncho that would cover her.

'Don't bother,' Aidan said bluntly. 'There's nothing you've got I haven't seen a hundred times before.'

Courtney scowled. 'I'm sure you're very well versed in female charms, Mr Sawyer.'

'Bodies anyway,' he agreed laconically, as he took another huge bite out of the banana. 'But if you want to try out some charms on me, I'm willing.'

'Don't hold your breath, Mr Sawyer.'

He shrugged. 'Suit yourself, but it'll be a long trip otherwise.'

'This is a business arrangement,' Courtney said firmly. 'No more, no less.'

She waited for him to dispute that. He didn't. He just shook his head, finished off the banana, then reached for some of the dried meat that Consuelo had packed. 'Want some?' He held a bit out to her.

She took it, popping it into her mouth. 'What is it?'

He grinned. 'Snake.'

She swallowed very slowly, taking care not to bat an eyelash. 'I didn't know you could dry snake meat,' she said with every bit of aplomb she could muster.

He burst out laughing. 'You're the most amazing woman.'

She doubted that was a compliment. 'Why?' she asked cautiously.

'Because...because nothing throws you! You can stare right through a naked man without batting an eye. You can just sit there getting soaked by a rainstorm, eating a banana as if you were at some high-class Paris café, and apparently you like snake!'

'Don't you?' she asked with mock sincerity.

'It's all right,' he conceded. He tilted his head. 'Do you really like it?' he asked after a moment.

'It's all right,' she echoed. 'But you told me no belly-aching. No complaining.'

'I didn't expect you to listen. You didn't listen to anything else I said.'

'I'm glad I didn't. I needed your help to find my parents.'

He sighed and leaned back against the side of the boat, stretching his legs out in front of him. 'They must be pretty special. Tell me about these parents of yours.' He was looking at her with more magnanimity than she had seen from him so far. It made her nervous. An interested Aiden Sawyer might be more trouble than a hostile one. She found him more attractive than he guessed. And the last thing she wanted was a little jungle romance. She watched him finishing off the meat, and cross his legs at the ankle. One hand rested on the engine cover. His scruffy damp khakis hid the muscular thighs now, but Courtney could remember well exactly what they looked like. Taking a deep breath she tried to drag her mind back to her parents.

'They are special people. Lovely people. Very devout. And very absent-minded, I fear. "Out of sight, out of mind" is their *modus operandi*.'

'You mean they might not remember you?'

'Oh, they'll remember me. And they'll be very glad to see me,' she predicted. 'But I shall be secondary to whatever else is going on in their lives.' She looked down, trailing her fingers through the water.

'Does that bother you?' He looked at her intently.

'No,' she said quickly. 'I prefer it that way. They run whatever they're involved in. It's better when it's not me.'

He gave her a wry, almost sympathetic grin. 'The voice of experience.'

'Yes.' Endicott Perkins was definitely a father who knew best.

'That why you ran away to the States?' he asked her.

She blinked, taken aback, momentarily bristling at the accusation. But she was also honest enough to admit its accuracy. 'Yes, I guess it is.' Her voice was purposely light. Then she turned the tables. 'What about you? What are you running away from?'

Aidan's face became an inscrutable mask. 'It's time for a siesta now,' he said abruptly. And without another word, he rolled up a poncho and pillowed his head on it, closing his eyes and shutting her out the way he shut out the sunlight.

Courtney watched him, more curious than ever. Obviously she had hit a nerve. What *was* he running away from? she wondered.

The possibilities nagged at her for the rest of the afternoon.

But further speculation came to naught. Aidan scarcely spoke from the time he finished his siesta until that evening when they had tied up in a tiny inlet where they would be camping for the night.

He fixed dinner in silence while Courtney watched. They ate in silence as well. It wasn't until he was rigging the hammocks that they spoke again. And it was because he had only rigged one that they spoke at all.

'Where's the other one?' Courtney demanded.

He turned and stared innocently at her. 'What other one?'

'Other hammock.'

'This is mine,' he offered. 'I'll hang yours wherever you like.' He waited expectantly, a hint of a smile on his face.

She waited, too. Then it began to dawn on her. Her eyes narrowed. 'You don't have another hammock?'

'Me?' Butter wouldn't have melted in his mouth.

Her teeth came together with a snap. 'You were to bring the provisions. That's your job.'

'Provisions.' He waved his arm in the direction of the food.

'A hammock is part of the provisions.'

He looked amazed. 'Oh? Where does it say that?'

Courtney exhaled sharply. They had signed no written contract. When she had questioned whether he would actually show up after agreeing to take her, he had looked offended. 'A man's word is his bond,' he had said stoutly. And so they had signed nothing. *Sucker,* she called herself.

'I'll be glad to share mine with you,' he told her. His smile became a full-fledged grin.

'Your magnanimity astonishes me.' She gave him a bitter smile in return. 'Thanks, but no thanks.' She unloaded one of the tarpaulins they had the food wrapped in.

He scowled at her. 'What the hell are you doing?'

'Making myself a bed.' She ignored him, spreading it out on the ground, then patting it. Bumps and lumps abounded. Grimacing, she picked it up and lugged it to the boat. That wouldn't be much better, but it wouldn't be quite so bumpy. And she would be in less danger of being trampled by a tapir either.

'You're crazy,' Aidan protested. 'This hammock is big enough for two.'

'Depends on the two,' Courtney replied. 'Not me and you.'

'You don't like me?' He sounded hurt.

She didn't deign to answer that. Instead she began rearranging the gear they had left in the bottom of the boat, trying to make herself something relatively unlumpy to stretch out on or curl up in. It wasn't going to be easy. Aidan stood on the riverbank and scowled at her. She ignored him. She hoped her parents appreciated her sufferings on their behalf.

'Goodnight,' she said when she had arranged her makeshift bed as best she could.

He grumbled something, then turned and stalked into the forest.

Sleeping was impossible. She could hear Aidan moving about, muttering. Once or twice she heard him come back down to the river, but she didn't turn her head to look at him. He would probably be smiling about her stupidity. She didn't want to see.

You could always sleep with him, she told herself as she punched one of the mesh bags she had stored clothes in into a more comfortable lump. Ha, she thought. That way lay disaster. However appealing he might be physically, he had no respect for her. And she didn't have much for him either. The last thing she wanted was an affair with a rowdy, manipulative jungle guide who was running away from his past.

'Damn it, get over here!' Aidan's voice suddenly broke into her thoughts.

She sat up with a jerk to find a flashlight in her face. 'Wha——?'

'I said, get out of that damned boat and come over here!'

'I'm trying to sleep.'

'Not there!'

She squinted into the light. 'Where, then?'

'Here.' His voice was gruff as he yanked her out of the boat and dragged her into the jungle where he had hung his hammock. He pointed the flashlight into the trees. A few feet from his hammock hung another one.

'I found one,' he muttered.

Courtney smiled, grateful for the darkness that hid it from him. 'Did you now?'

'Yes, damn it.' He grabbed her around the waist and thrust her into it before she could say another word. Then he draped it with mosquito netting. When he had finished, he eased himself into his own.

The soft sounds of the night-time jungle washed over them.

Courtney yawned and stretched, luxuriating in the gentle swaying of her new bed. 'Thank you, Aidan,' she said softly.

He grunted and rolled over. 'Can't blame a guy for trying,' he mumbled.

*　　*　　*

He woke her at dawn. 'Come on, Bo-Peep, rise and shine. Time to get a move on.'

Courtney peered blearily up at him, unsure that she had even slept. But she must have, for she remembered dreams filled with monsters, beasties, and a brave little girl taking on a particularly wolfish one. It wasn't hard to find the symbolism there.

'Coming,' she mumbled, rolling out of the hammock. All around she heard a zeet-zeet sound, like tiny saws cutting wood. 'Is that frogs?' she asked Aidan.

'Mm-hm. Poisonous arrow frogs. Courting.'

'Courting?'

'You do know what that is, don't you, Bo-Peep?' he grinned.

She scowled, ignoring him, trying to drag a brush through her damp, snarled hair.

'Have you done it?'

She blinked. 'Done what?'

'Courted? Got a boyfriend?'

'I did. It wasn't serious. What about you?' she turned the tables.

Aidan shook his head. 'Not me. Courting leads to marriage. The last thing I want is to get married.'

Which told her exactly what she had expected about him. He was a no-strings-attached man. And, since he was, she had better stay well away from him. She finished with her hair, then said, 'I'll be right back,' and disappeared into the jungle to deal with more personal things.

Aidan was already sitting in the stern of the boat by the time she had got her hammock and all her gear ready. He waited silently, probably expecting her to ask him to help her pack it. She didn't. She wasn't going to ask him for anything. Not even a cup of Consuelo's strong, sweet *cafezinho* or something else that would prise her eyes open before they set out.

Today even more than yesterday she was conscious of his eyes on her. Once she offered to sit in the stern and take a turn guiding the boat downriver, but he declined.

'I like the view from here.'

'That's what I was afraid of,' she said tartly, and he laughed. He had quite a view, and she would be the first to admit it. The periodic rains kept her shirt damp and revealing all the time. And one shirt was just as bad as the other. The poncho was a dead loss. It retained all the moisture in the air and about twice as much heat besides. She felt as if she were taking a steam bath when she put it on. After fifteen minutes she rolled it up and stowed it in the bottom of the boat, acknowledging its uselessness. But she didn't complain.

They ate lunch during a rainstorm just as they had the day before. Only this time there was no small talk. Aidan was silent, concentrating on his food. Once or twice she caught him looking at her, but if she caught his eye, he looked away. It was almost as if he were avoiding her, rather than the other way around.

Curiouser and curiouser, she thought.

Now and then, in an effort to try to initiate a normal conversation, she would ask him a question. She asked him how long he had been in the jungle. He said five years and ignored her next one which was where he had come from.

'We're not playing twenty questions,' he snapped irritably.

After that, she left him alone.

Clearly the man had a problem. Perhaps he had murdered someone, she thought. Or perhaps he was a forger. A counterfeiter. A spy. More likely, she told herself, he was a divorced husband who had run out on his alimony payments. She wondered what sort of woman Aidan Sawyer would marry.

That line of thought brought her up short. Irritably she reminded herself that she had no business wondering any such thing! Nor did she care at all!

Nevertheless, she was almost relieved when he cut the engine abruptly, interfering with her train of thought.

'Are we stopping?' Her watch said it was only about four in the afternoon. Last night they hadn't stopped until after six.

He shook his head. 'Not yet. We're getting into Indian territory hereabouts.'

'How can you tell?'

'Listen.'

She did, but all she detected were the sounds of the river, birds—thousands of birds—and some insistent background rhythm. Did he mean that? She wasn't sure. Her ears weren't attuned to the environment. They still expected car horns, the roar of airplanes, the screech of brakes, and the drone of the television she had left back home. She shook her head.

'I don't hear anything.'

'Well, I do,' he said. 'And it's better to paddle than go through with the motor.' His look dared her to dispute his decision.

She didn't. Having spent her early days living among various Indian tribes, she respected them. And she respected Aidan's decision now. 'Hand me a paddle,' she said. 'I'll help.'

His dark brows lifted. 'What? No argument?'

'No argument.' She held out her hand. 'The paddle, Mr Sawyer?'

He still looked at her sceptically, but he handed it to her without further comment.

She was glad for something to do. The rhythmic movement as she paddled made a counterpoint to the darting watchfulness of her eyes as she scanned the riverbanks. Aidan hummed softly, as if he were simply driving to the supermarket for a pint of milk. But Courtney didn't feel nearly that blasé.

The thrashing of a tapir as it lumbered through the jungle and heaved itself into the river startled her. So did the skittering of the monkeys that swung through the branches overhead.

'Relax,' Aidan said finally, his voice calm, soothing almost, as if he were a parent reassuring a frightened child.

'I am relaxed,' Courtney retorted sharply. And she was fairly successful in believing that as time passed, because she never saw a thing.

She was astonished, in fact, when she heard Aidan murmur, 'Uh-huh,' as if he had just had his suspicions confirmed.

'Uh-huh what?' She shifted to look at him over her shoulder.

He nodded slightly, his eyes flickering towards the far bank where she couldn't see a thing. 'They're over there. Just keep on paddling and don't get hyper.'

'Of course not!'

But all the same, she wasn't prepared for the way her heart stopped when they rounded the next bend, and seven young men with bowl haircuts and red and black face-paint stood on the riverbank, spears and blowguns aimed directly at them.

CHAPTER FOUR

COURTNEY froze.

'Smile,' Aidan commanded. His voice was like padded steel. And as he spoke, he dipped his paddle once more into the water, turning the boat and sending them skimming directly towards the bank slightly upstream of the silent men.

Her heart in her throat, Courtney smiled.

Aidan eased the boat around so that he was between her and the men on the shore. His movements were easy, controlled and, she noticed, he kept both hands visible at all times. He spoke to the men softly. His slightly nasal words rang a bell in Courtney's memory, but meant nothing to her now.

They meant something to the Indians, though. One of them stepped forward slightly and nodded. He reached down and took hold of the rope Aidan handed him, then passed it to another of the men. Together they pulled until the boat was firmly aground.

Courtney didn't move. She sat quietly and waited. Once she would have been thrust forward. Now she had simply to wait and be silent. It was Aidan's place to conduct their affairs. Thank God, she thought.

She kept her eyes cast down. To stare would be belligerent, disrespectful. But she couldn't help catching the interested looks on the faces of a couple of the men when she glanced up for a brief second. When she offered a fledgling smile, one of them gave her a wink that wasn't difficult to interpret even with the language barrier. Some things were the same no matter what culture you were in. She looked away quickly.

Aidan gave her a worried glance, then turned his attention to the man who had stepped forward and began to speak with him. They both used their hands, gesturing as they spoke. The Indian pointed off into the jungle. Aidan shook his head and asked a question. The other man paused, then nodded. He said something to one of his companions, the man who had winked at Courtney. He gave her another assessing look, then grinned and vanished into the woods without a sound.

No one spoke until he returned and motioned for them to follow.

Aidan turned to Courtney. 'Come on.' He held out his hand to her. She looked at it warily for a moment before she put hers in it and stepped out of the boat. Expecting that he would release her when her feet hit the ground, she was surprised when strong, callused fingers closed over hers, and he drew her with him as he followed the leader of the Indian men into the jungle. She felt more than saw him glance down at her, as if he expected her to bolt. Once upon a time she would have wanted to. But now she simply kept her head down and went on walking.

They had gone no more than a hundred yards through what at first seemed impenetrable jungle when they reached a circle of a dozen huts. The outer walls and heavy roof thatch overlapped, protecting the village from outsiders, but the men led Aidan and Courtney through a break in the wall to the clearing within. There, several children romped about, most wearing nothing, though one, Courtney noted, had *'Mazatlán'* written on the front of his torn T-shirt, and another wore a relic that said 'UC Berkeley'. Anthropological cast-offs, she decided, and smiled at the children who stopped playing and regarded the two newcomers curiously.

The leader spoke again to Aidan, who nodded, stopping where he was.

'He's getting the chief,' Aidan explained quietly as the man disappeared into one of the huts, leaving them standing with the other men, the children, and one or two young women staring at them shyly. 'To welcome us.'

'You know the chief?'

'I've met him once or twice. He'll probably invite us to stay. If he does, we're taking him up on it,' he continued firmly, as if he expected an argument.

He wasn't going to get one. 'Suits me.' Courtney thought that having a tribe of Indians around was a good idea. Spending another night in the jungle alone with Aidan seemed far more dangerous. It was too unpredictable. Or, perhaps, it was its very predictability that worried her.

There was a flurry of movement just then, and the man who had gone into the hut stepped out, then moved aside for the chief.

The chief, Courtney realised, was not much taller than she was. A stocky, heavily muscled man of indeterminate age, he seemed unsurprised to see Aidan, but his eyes widened when they settled on her. He looked from Aidan to Courtney and back again.

Courtney heard Aidan mutter something incomprehensible under his breath. Then he stepped forward, smiling, holding his palms out.

The chief smiled back. *'Bom día, o meu amigo,'* he said, surprising Courtney with soft, slow Portuguese she could understand. 'You have come back.'

'Just passing through,' Aidan assured him.

'I hear of scientists,' the chief said. 'You come ahead of them.'

Aidan shook his head, glancing down at Courtney who deliberately looked away. 'Not me.'

'You're not guiding them?' the chief asked, frowning.

Aidan shook his head. 'I had another commitment.'

The chief looked at Courtney also and raised his eyebrows. Aidan nodded, his smile widening. He took Courtney's hand again. She started to pull away, but he hung on grimly.

'A sua novia,' the chief said. It wasn't a question.

His *girlfriend?* Courtney bristled. 'I'm no——' she began, but Aidan cut her off.

'You could say that. We——'

The chief beamed. 'We have just the place for you.' He pointed to one of the huts. 'You may have this, the two of you.'

'Thank you,' Aidan said at the same time Courtney blurted,

'Not on your life!'

She said it in English, and no one but Aidan understood her words. But the man who had winked at her frowned for a moment, as if he caught the gist of it if not the actual words.

Aidan expelled a long, angry breath. 'Come on!' He practically jerked her off her feet as he hauled her into the hut that the chief had designated. Sticking his head back out, he said, *'Muito obrigado,'* to the chief, then ducked back in and glared at her.

'What the hell were you trying to do?'

'Me?' She was outraged. *'You* let them think I was your woman.'

'So?'

'So?' She yelped. 'I am not your woman, and I will not spend the night in this hut with you!'

He sighed disgustedly. 'I suppose you think I'm going to attack you.'

'I have reason to!'

'What reason?' His voice was scathing.

'Last night,' she reminded him sweetly. 'The hammock trick.'

Aidan's eyes rolled heavenwards. 'That's not the same thing.'

'No?'

'No.'

'Well, pardon me if I don't see the difference.'

'Listen, you stupid female, I am trying to save your hide. Women without protectors are fair game. You'll be safer with me.'

Courtney snorted inelegantly. 'You've been watching too many old movies, Mr Sawyer. That's the most ridiculous thing I've ever heard.'

'You have a better idea?' Scepticism dripped from his voice.

'You bet I do.'

Even his argument that he was just protecting her infuriated her—not that she believed it for a minute. It was just another example of men always thinking they knew best. If Aidan Sawyer thought he could just step in and run her life for her, he had another think coming. *Men!* They were all alike. First her father, then Clarke, now Aidan!

She wasn't sure which made her maddest—that he was trying to coerce her into sleeping with him or that he was using such an underhand means of doing so. He hadn't even told the chief why they were there, for heaven's sake! The chief might even know her father. Without another word, she stalked back out of the hut and looked around.

Several of the men from the group who had met them were standing not far away, their gazes straying to the hut she had just come out of. The one who had winked was talking softly, the others were grinning or laughing. Their grins widened when they saw Courtney.

She brushed her hair back away from her face and looked around once more for the chief. Not seeing him, she approached the men.

'Me-desculpe,' she said nervously, directing her words to the one who had been talking, *'Eu necesito falar com o chefe.'*

He jerked his head towards the hut the chief had come out of.

'Courtney!' Aidan appeared in the doorway, scowling.

But before he could stop her, she darted into the hut the man had pointed out. The chief was squatting on the floor of the hut. His initial surprise at seeing the intruder was obvious, though he schooled his features almost immediately. He rose slowly so that they were looking eye to eye, his expression forbidding.

Courtney gulped, then reminded herself of the alternative. 'Pardon me,' she began, rediscovering her

Portuguese as she went along. 'I—I need your help. My name is Courtney Perkins, and I'm looking for my father.' She paused, hoping he understood. He didn't indicate that he had one way or the other, so she blundered on. 'I hoped you might know him. Endicott Perkins. He's a missionary.'

She held her breath when she said that. There were Indians who had no use for missionaries. There were Indians who killed them. There were missionaries, she was willing to admit, who might deserve it. Not her father, though. Endicott Perkins was generally respected, even loved. He didn't 'preach at' so much as 'live with' the people who were his mission in life. Still...

'En-di-cott?' The chief's sober face broke into a wide grin. *'Sim, sim. Eu o conheço bem. E voce é a sua filha?'*

Courtney nodded, smiling herself. 'Yes. Yes, I'm his daughter. That's why I've come. I need to find my parents. And Mr Sawyer——' she paused significantly and looked towards the door beyond which she was sure he was lurking '—is only helping me find them. He's my guide, not my *novio.'*

The chief's eyes widened. 'Ah. *Guia.'* He raised his eyebrows as if asking for confirmation.

'Sim,' Courtney assured him. 'My guide.' She repeated it in English, Portuguese and Spanish, just to make sure he understood.

'So——' he grinned at her '—you do not wish to share a hammock, yes?'

'Yes. I mean, no. No hammock. Please. No hut, if possible.'

'I understand.' He stuck his head out of the hut again, saying something to the woman who was apparently just going to string the hammock. She looked from Courtney to Aidan and back again, then giggled. The men who were standing about snickered.

Aidan himself, leaning against one of the supports to the hut, scowled at her. *Serves you right,* she thought and gave him a smug smile in return.

*   *   *

'He knows my father,' she said to him the next time she spoke to him alone just as they were preparing to eat with the chief and his family. 'He can help us find him. I don't know why you didn't ask.' She paused. 'No, that's not true, is it? I know very well why you didn't.' She shook her head and patted him condescendingly on the forearm. 'Tough luck.'

Aidan just grunted and shook his head as if she had just done something very stupid.

But she would have been far stupider, she thought, to let him get away with trying to sleep with her.

They ate cooked plantains and some kind of meat, Courtney wasn't sure what, for supper. There was much joking and talking, none of which she understood. Aidan, however, appeared to understand a part of it. She saw him cast a sidelong glance at her once or twice after one of the men whispered something to another. But she just gave him a blithe smile in return. He needn't try to make her feel threatened. It was quite clear that the chief held Endicott Perkins in the highest esteem. He wasn't about to mistreat such a revered man's daughter.

In fact, she was treated like royalty all evening long. He struggled to speak to her in Portuguese once the meal was over. And Courtney took great pains to answer him. He asked about her life, if she had a husband, children. And he seemed shocked when she said she didn't.

'But you are old,' he protested, looking askance.

Aidan snickered. Courtney glared at him.

'Not old by our standards,' she said. 'Twenty-two is not old.'

'Yes. Yes, very old,' the chief insisted. 'White dolly born the year of the flood. My daughter born the year we kill the jaguars.' He looked at Aidan for help in judging the difference in their ages.

'She's five years younger than you are,' Aidan told Courtney.

'Five years,' the chief said. 'And look.' He pointed to the woman who must be his daughter. She had a child hanging on to her who looked about four. Another was nursing from her breast. Courtney swallowed. 'And this one——' the chief picked up a little boy about two '—is her son, too. So what do you have?'

Courtney didn't imagine that the mangy tomcat she had rescued from starvation last winter would count for much.

'Tell him about the bunny books, sweetheart,' Aidan suggested, grinning.

She shot him a malevolent glance. 'You should talk,' she said. 'Mr Footloose.'

His expression darkened. 'I was married once,' he said curtly. Then he turned his back on her and began to talk to the man next to him.

They didn't speak again for the rest of the evening. Many of the Indians turned in not long after the sun had set. But a few continued to talk on, squatting beside the ever-present fire, laughing softly. One of the men got out a reed flute and began to play. Courtney yawned. The chief's daughter giggled.

'You sleep?' she asked Courtney in halting Portuguese. Courtney nodded.

'Come.' The girl shifted the baby to her hip and, with the four-year-old and the two-year-old trailing after her, she led Courtney to a hut across the round. She touched a newly hung hammock. 'Here you sleep,' she said. 'Only old woman here. No bother you.'

Courtney nodded and thanked her. She touched the hair of the two little boys and one of them shyly touched her shirt. Then the family turned and walked back to the fire. The girl said something to one of the younger men, probably her husband, and he got up to join her. They disappeared into one of the huts, arms around each other. Courtney's throat tightened as she watched them go. She felt unaccountably bereft, lonely, turning back to her hammock alone.

Maybe you wanted to share with Aidan Sawyer after all? she asked herself scornfully. No. It wasn't indiscriminate sex that she wanted. It was closeness, sharing. And could she have got that from Aidan? Not a chance.

Courtney could still see him sitting beside the fire. He was half sprawled, not squatting like the men he was talking with. The firelight flickered, lighting then shadowing the angles of his face. It was darker now with the addition of two days' growth of beard. But it was, she acknowledged, even more attractive than before. It was a pity actually, that she wasn't the sort to go in for affairs. He would be a beaut.

But she would be a lifetime getting over it. So she turned resolutely back to the hammock the chief's daughter had shown her and, kicking off her shoes, rolled herself into it. Across the way the old woman was already asleep. Her snores were quite audible above the voices she could still hear outside. But they were far less likely to keep Courtney awake than Aidan's softer ones had the night before.

She smiled, thinking of his chagrin when she had foiled his single hammock attempt. Poor Aidan. Well, perhaps he would find another woman to share with him. One of the women who had been lurking on the edges of the conversation all evening, perhaps? The thought was less pleasing than she would have wished.

Don't think about him, she told herself. Think about tomorrow, about finding Dad and Mom. Think about anything but Aidan Sawyer...even bunnies if you must! She smiled and closed her eyes. In seconds, she was asleep.

She wasn't sure what woke her.

The constant soft scuttling sounds in the roof thatch were a part of the background now. As long as she didn't think about what was making them, she was fine. And the old woman's snores continued unabated. But all at once Courtney felt a stab of fear, an unnamed apprehension. She lay perfectly still in her hammock, not even breathing. Her ears were attuned to anything odd, anything strange. But for long moments there was nothing.

Then she heard it again. A soft thrush-thrush. Then silence. Then the same noise again, slow and barely discernible. Bare feet.

She turned over, feigning restless sleep. Through slitted eyes she could still see the fire through the hut opening. It had burned down, no more now than glowing coals and embers casting everything into shadow. And two of the shadows were moving—one several yards behind the other.

She bit down on her lower lip, watching intently. Perhaps they were simply hunters getting an early start. But they didn't move like hunters. Or rather, they moved like hunters closing in on the kill, she thought frantically. And they were coming directly towards her!

She squeezed her eyes tight shut and the faint glow behind her eyelids that had been there moments before because of the firelight was suddenly gone. The first man stood in the doorway of the hut. She could hear the quick, heavy rasp of his breathing. The smell of wood smoke and human sweat invaded her nostrils. She twisted away in the hammock, still trying to feign sleep. He moved again, and a strong hand touched her arm.

She jerked, opening her mouth to protest. A hand closed over it. Her eyes flew open and she found herself staring into the hungry eyes of the man who had met the boat yesterday, the one who had winked at her.

He was smiling now, keeping his hand over her mouth while the other stroked her arm, her stomach, her breasts. He murmured something to her softly, something that was supposed to soothe her and calm her no doubt.

Courtney shivered, trying to shrink inside herself, to get away from him while she thought what to do. She reached up to push his hand away. Afraid of crying out. Afraid of offending. Afraid of what would happen if she did. Afraid of what would happen if she didn't!

He bent his head closer to her, then removed his hand from her mouth and replaced it with his own, his lips hard on hers. Abruptly fear of offending vanished. She grabbed for his arm to push him away when all of a sudden he jerked away of his own accord.

She stared, bug-eyed in the darkness, as she discovered that it hadn't been of his own accord at all. He had been yanked backward at the same time as a hand closed over his mouth and a fist came around and drove itself into his belly.

'Ooof.'

'Damn.' She heard the muffled curse, then saw that the interloper had been spun around and socked once more. In the jaw this time. His head whipped back and he slumped to the ground.

'Don't just lie there, for God's sake,' Aidan's voice snapped at her. 'Get your butt out of that hammock and get your gear. I'll be back for you in a minute.'

Hoisting the unconscious man over his shoulder, he staggered back out of the hut leaving Courtney to stare after him.

In seconds everything was back to normal. The shrill sounds of tree frogs, the snores of the old woman, the unending rush of the river in the distance. It might as well never have happened.

She shook her head, half thinking it was all a bad dream. Had a man actually touched her, stroked her? And had Aidan suddenly appeared like an avenging angel and——

'I said, get moving,' Aidan hissed. He was back, looming in the doorway, cutting off her light. It hadn't been a dream. 'Or would you rather I'd let him have his way with you?'

'He wasn't——'

'He damned well was! And I'm not standing around arguing about it.' He was bending over, stuffing whatever he could see that belonged to Courtney into her duffel bag. Then, shouldering it, he turned and tipped her out of the hammock on to the ground.

'Come on,' he growled and set off across the round without looking back.

She scrambled to her feet, rubbing her bottom where it had hit the hard-packed floor. Then, unsure of whether she was going from the frying pan into the fire, she hurried after him.

He stalked quietly through the forest, his pace quick. Courtney had almost to run to keep up with him. He led her unerringly back to the river, untied the boat and waited until she got in, then shoved it off and climbed in after her. He thrust a paddle in her hands and took the other in his own. Then he propelled them swiftly out into the main channel. Within minutes they had left the village far behind them.

He didn't speak to her until they had put about an hour between themselves and the village. Then he eased up on the paddling long enough to button his shirt. Noting the sudden change in their speed, Courtney turned around to look at him.

'That's one,' he said.

One? She stared at him blankly.

He gave her a bitter smile. 'You remember, sweetheart. We had a little discussion about how you were going to be responsible for yourself, about how I wasn't going to have to get you out of jams.'

Courtney glowered at him. How like him to say, 'I told you so.' 'It was your fault,' she told him bluntly.

He stared. '*My fault?* How the hell do you figure that? It never would have happened if you'd done what I arranged in the first place and stayed with me.'

'It was because you arranged it that I didn't!'

'Huh?' He blinked. 'Run that by me again.'

'You tried to manipulate me into going to bed with you,' she accused him furiously.

And she was even more furious a moment later when he merely shrugged. 'You would've been safer.'

Oh, yeah? she wondered. She wouldn't have bet on it. 'I didn't like the way you did it,' she told him.

He gave her a wry look. 'There was a better way? Would you have done it if I'd asked you?'

'Gone to bed with you? Of course not.'

'Forget going to bed with me, damn it! Would you have stayed with me?'

'No,' she said flatly.

'Then maybe you can understand why I did what I did.'

She glared. 'That doesn't excuse it. I don't like being manipulated!'

'Neither do I.' He gave her a hard stare. 'You beat me hands down in the manipulation department, sweetheart. Who got us here in the first place?'

There was no way to answer that.

Aidan dipped his paddle in the water, never taking his eyes off her, letting the full implications of his words sink in. They did, making Courtney increasingly uncomfortable.

Finally she scowled and said, 'We're even, then.'

'We'll see about that.'

'The chief respected my father,' she said stubbornly. 'He respected *me*. I thought it would be all right.'

'Yeah.' Aidan gave her a sardonic grin. 'But at least one of those guys respected your body more.'

Courtney was glad it was still quite dark. Aidan didn't need to see how pink her face had become. 'I'm sorry,' she said at last and with great reluctance, her voice gruff. 'I didn't try to entice him.'

'That wasn't a little come-on smile I witnessed?' Aidan raised an eyebrow. His scepticism would have been evident even on a moonless night. 'That one when you were still in the boat.'

'It certainly wasn't intentional, Mr Sawyer,' she said sharply. 'I was being pleasant.'

His immediate bark of laughter showed what he thought of that. 'Right. Our very own Miss Manners.'

Courtney gave up. There was no use talking to the stubborn idiot. He would think whatever he wanted, no matter what she said. She concentrated on being as unobtrusive as possible for the remainder of the day. And Aidan seemed to like it like that.

*   *   *

They paddled in silence until daybreak. Then he cut in the engine and they made better time. They ran into one group of Indians scouting along the river shortly before midday and before Courtney could say a word, Aidan said, 'Keep your eyes down and your mouth shut.'

Having learned that polite smiles were capable of mis-interpretation, she did as he said, only bristling at him afterwards, 'You could have said please.'

'I could have,' he agreed, 'but I don't see why I should. You aren't the pretty please type.'

Courtney didn't want to know what 'type' he thought she was, but she was sure it would be unflattering in the extreme. She ignored the insult and went back to trying to ignore him as well.

At lunch she helped with food when he asked her to, and later on she didn't complain when they continued travelling far into the evening because he decided that he didn't want to camp where the Indians had reported seeing miners.

He didn't explain why, but she could guess. If one lusty Indian had considered her fair game, she could im-agine what a camp full of miners would think.

When at last he did find an area that might be suitable for camping, several miles downriver from the mining area, he tied the boat up, then made his way several yards into the jungle until he found a satisfactory spot. There he hung both hammocks in silence, then bent to start a fire.

'Want some help?' Courtney asked him. It was the first time she had spoken to him since lunch. Silence had seemed the better part of survival. He had spoken barely ten words since he had bawled her out in the morning, and she thought if she started a conversation she might incur his wrath further. But he looked less fierce to-night. His scowl had vanished, and he looked more tired than anything else.

Not surprising, she thought, considering that he probably hadn't got any sleep the night before. He had obviously stayed up waiting for her amorous visitor to make his move. She felt a momentary twinge of something like guilt.

'You can sort out some grub.' He jerked his head in the direction of the food pack. 'I'm going down to the river to have a bath.'

He plucked a clean shirt and a towel out of his pack, started down the path to the river, then stopped and came back. 'Here.' He rummaged beneath the packs and came up with the rifle, holding it out to her.

Courtney blanched. 'What's that for?'

'Protection,' he said succinctly.

'You think those miners we heard about might...' Her voice trailed off. There were some things she didn't want to talk about. Not after last night.

'I damned well don't know what to think, sweetheart. I just know I'd rather you were prepared.'

'I——'

'You *can* shoot, can't you?'

'Yes. But I'd rather not...'

'I'd rather not, too. But you don't always get the choice, do you?' he asked her.

Numbly she shook her head.

'Then just use it if you have to.' And with those ominous words, he turned his back on her and disappeared into the jungle.

Courtney didn't bother to watch him go. She leaned the rifle carefully against a tree trunk, made sure the safety-catch was on, and set about getting dinner. It wasn't going to be gourmet fare. But the selection would be better than they had expected by tonight because they had saved food yesterday when they had eaten with the Indians.

Remembering the experience, she felt nervous again. The soft scufflings in the trees above and the occasional rustlings on the jungle floor, which usually were no more than background noise, unnerved her now. She glanced over her shoulder warily, but saw nothing.

She put a small can of stew on the fire to heat, then added some plantains wrapped in leaves and embers. She opened a tin of sardines and hacked off several slices of the bread that Consuelo had made for them to take along. Then she got out the grapes that she had picked earlier while Aidan was swimming.

The tree frogs went suddenly silent.

She dropped the grapes on the ground, whirling around to see if she was in danger. Nothing. Except a bunch of muddy grapes.

Damn. She wiped at them with a handkerchief, but to no avail. She would just have to wash them off. Readjusting the can on the fire so that it wouldn't burn while she was gone, she started down the trail towards the river, then remembered the gun. If Aidan saw her without it, he would have a fit.

Let him, she thought. Then with a shiver she remembered the feel of that man's unwanted touch the night before. Maybe she ought to take it. Just in case. She went back and got it, then headed back towards the river.

The jungle was still silent. Waiting. It felt eerie, quiet. It was a relief to hear the sounds of Aidan splashing just out of sight. It would be better, too, if she kept him out of sight. He wouldn't want her interrupting his bath. Not, she thought wryly, unless she planned to take one with him. And since she had no intention of doing that, she cut off the path and moved downstream a little distance so that she wouldn't bother him.

She pretended great absorption in washing off the grapes. But she couldn't stop her eyes drifting towards where she heard him splashing. And she couldn't help edging closer and finally staring through the foliage once she had.

The river curved slightly, so she was out of sight behind thick foliage that went clear to the water's edge. But Aidan was bathing on the narrow sandbar where they had tied up the boat and he wasn't hard to see beneath the overhanging branches.

The sight of him took her breath away. Tall, tanned all over and gorgeous, he stood in water to mid-thigh while he soaped his chest and arms and belly.

Courtney swallowed, blinked, told herself to look away, but couldn't. She was transfixed, enchanted by the pure masculine beauty of him. He finished soaping himself, and she saw him sink slowly down into the water, submerging completely. Ripples fanned out from where he had vanished. She waited, watching, leaning forward, worried when he didn't reappear at once. Her fingers tightened on the gun. Where was he?

Just then he broke the surface far closer to her than he had been, and she sucked in her breath. He stood and shook the water out of his hair and eyes, then began moving towards the bank. Courtney suddenly remembered that she had better get back to the camp before he did. One last look, she promised, and parted the leaves that obscured her view.

He was no more than thirty feet from her now, towelling his hair, water streaming off the rest of his body, making glistening tracks through the matted hair on his chest. Courtney's eyes followed the tracks, the sight of him making her ache, heating her blood.

A sudden scurrying and chattering of monkeys made her glance up, and then her blood ran cold.

There in the tree just above Aidan hunched a jaguar, waiting. Ready to spring. It inched out on the limb, looking down, eyes fixed on the man below.

Courtney's breath caught in her throat. God, no! She felt a scream rising in her throat and forced it down again. To shout would be the worst thing she could do. But then, how to warn him?

Her fingers gripped the cold steel of the gun. Warning wasn't possible. Even if he knew, what could he do? Instead she dropped the grapes gently to the ground and released the safety-catch on the rifle. Then she lifted it, resting the butt of the rifle against her shoulder and aiming the barrel at the animal in the tree. She hadn't lied when she had told Aidan she could shoot. But she hadn't told him it had been years since she had done it, either. Perhaps it would come back to her, like riding a bicycle or knitting. She could only hope.

Gritting her teeth and bracing her feet, she pulled the trigger.

CHAPTER FIVE

AIDAN never knew what hit him.

At first Courtney thought she had. The sharp report of the rifle made him jerk upwards, his arms flung out. Then the jaguar crashed from the tree, knocking him senseless to the ground.

'Oh, God.' Courtney scrambled through the bushes, then slowed her pace and approached man and animal cautiously. She kept the rifle pointed down, though she remained ready to use it again if the jaguar moved. It didn't.

Neither did Aidan for several moments. Then at last she heard him groan and saw him twitch in the dirt, muttering and trying to heave the great weight of the jaguar off him. Relief flooded through her, and she checked the rifle, making sure the safety-catch was on it. Then, dropping it to the ground, she ran and knelt beside him.

'Are you all right?'

'Wh——' Still stunned, Aidan rolled over, trying to focus on her, wiping the mud from his mouth.

She bent over him, using all her strength to haul the jaguar off. 'Are you hurt?'

Aidan blinked—first at her, then at the body of the jaguar lying beside him dead. He shook his head slowly, as if he needed to clear it, needed to make sense of what had just happened, not as if he meant he wasn't hurt. He was filthy again, she could see that. Dirty from being thrown to the mud by the impact. And scowling.

'What the hell did you do?' he demanded roughly, levering himself up on his elbows.

'I . . . shot it.'

'You shot it?'

'It...it was...going to...' she swallowed, feeling suddenly dizzy '...get you.'

Aidan looked from her to the dead jaguar. The full import of the situation seemed gradually to be coming into focus. He wiped a hand across his face, then closed his eyes. When he opened them again the jaguar still lay there motionless and the white-faced woman staring down at him still looked as if she might faint at any moment. And when he thought about what had almost happened, he thought he might too. It terrified him, and he took refuge in anger.

'What the hell were you doing there, anyway?'

Courtney's gaze, which had drifted to the jaguar to avoid Aidan's nakedness, jerked back to meet the blazing fire of his eyes. 'Washing grapes.'

'Grapes! What the——'

'They...they fell in the mud. I brought them down to wash them off. I didn't want to come right where you were swimming. So I came downstream a little.'

'And you just happened to be watching me anyway.'

Her pale face got a bit of colour at the accuracy of that, but she shook her head fiercely. 'You just...just popped up right on the other side of these bushes when I was...going back. I...I heard a noise and...I looked up and...there it was.'

She didn't need to say any more. They both knew what would have happened if she hadn't used the gun.

Their eyes met. His were deep green and serious. All the scorn and mockery she was used to seeing in them was absent now.

'Thanks,' he muttered finally, his voice shaking. He struggled to his feet and reached for the towel, aware now of his nakedness. 'I need to wash off.'

'Yes.' But this time she didn't have any qualms about hanging around. She sat on the edge of a fallen tree, cradling the gun across her knees, and waited for him. If he wished she would leave, he didn't say so. He submerged completely again, though not for as long a time as he had earlier. Then he began to swim back upstream towards his clothes.

Courtney stood up, fetched the grapes and, shouldering the gun, followed him. He was stepping into his trousers when she got there. She politely averted her eyes while he zipped and snapped, though there was nothing now she hadn't seen before and they both knew it. Then, as she started back towards the camp, he said, 'Wait.'

'What is it? Are you OK?'

He still looked pale and a little shaky. That made two of them, Courtney thought. But he had more right to than she did. He was, after all, the one who had almost died.

'I'm OK,' he assured her. 'But I'm not letting that cat go to waste. I can't leave it here. Every hungry carnivore in the jungle will be on top of us if I do. Come on.' And he went back downstream the way they came, intent on skinning and cutting up the jaguar where it lay. It was heavy. Over two hundred pounds, Courtney guessed. There was no way he could bring it along to their camp.

He stood looking at it a moment as if contemplating once more the near disaster he had just survived. His eyes went from the one gunshot wound in its head to the woman with the rifle who stood watching him. 'I guess you can shoot,' he said wryly. 'Those miners were lucky they didn't come around.'

'I was lucky I hit it.' She didn't feel heroic, just shaky now that it was over.

Aidan shook his head. '*I* was lucky you hit it,' he said grimly and, getting out his knife, he set to work. Courtney lingered, watching, turning her head at the sight of the blood. But then she thought how much worse it would have been if it had been Aidan's blood she was looking at. 'I'll help,' she said.

He gave her a long look, and she had no idea what he was thinking. But he got out a smaller knife and told her what to do. She took it, swallowed hard, and set to work.

They brought enough meat back to camp to use that day and the day after. Beyond that it would spoil, Aidan said. He pressed her into helping him drag it to the boat.

'What are you going to do?'

'Take it over to the other side of the river. The smell of blood attracts other animals. I think we've had enough for one night.'

'Me, too,' Courtney said with heartfelt enthusiasm as she helped him haul the carcass on board. Then she waited, glancing nervously at the treetops while Aidan rowed across the river. She saw nothing, but she was still relieved when he returned and they were on their way to camp again.

The can of stew had burned, but Aidan took two of the jaguar steaks and prepared to cook them.

'It's a good thing you killed it,' he tried joking when he looked at the incinerated can, 'or we'd have gone hungry.'

'If that...that *cat* hadn't been there,' Courtney said sharply, still unable to see any humour in such a narrow escape, 'I'd have got back before it burned.'

'I know.' His voice was soft, and she almost regretted her sharp tone. No one knew better than Aidan how close he had come to a grisly death. He did not need her seriousness to remind him.

'Here,' she said, reaching for the meat he was about to put on the fire. 'I'll do it. You rest.'

He looked as if he might protest. But she didn't give him the chance, taking the meat and putting it on two skewers, then balancing it over the fire with the aid of two supporting forked sticks. She set out the bread and the plantains that were almost too well cooked and finally she opened a tin of sardines. It might not be gourmet fare, but it would do. She turned to say so to Aidan and found him leaning back in his hammock, his eyes closed, his face still tense.

For the first time she thought Aidan Sawyer looked as if he might have a smidgen of vulnerability. He had a right to it, she figured. He had had a long, hard day.

He didn't move as she dished up the plantains, some of the sardines, the grapes, and took the cooked jaguar meat off the fire. She was almost loath to wake him. But it had been hours since they had eaten, and it seemed a waste to let the food go uneaten.

'How's this?' she asked him at last, holding out a plate.

He opened his eyes slowly, looking disorientated for a moment. Then coming to, he nodded. 'Thanks.' He took the plate from her and, grimacing from some undoubtedly bruised muscles, sat up and began to eat.

They ate in silence, both of them ravenous, the near brush with death having given them an appetite, an appreciation for being alive. But there was more to it than that. There was a sense of harmony now. Although Courtney was conscious of his eyes on her all the time—a not unusual occurrence—for the first time she didn't sense the overt hostility that had existed between them on every other occasion.

Perhaps, she thought, if she saved his life every day they might become friends.

Could she be friends with Aidan Sawyer? Did she even want to be? For all its appeal, it was a dangerous idea.

And it got even more dangerous when the coffee had boiled, and she poured them each a cup. When she added a spoonful of sugar and handed it to him, he smiled at her.

Without warning, her heart began to sing.

No, she thought frantically, *don't.* But her heart ignored her, too enchanted by the pair of tired, bloodshot green eyes that smiled at her and the lopsided grin in the whiskery face to pay attention to her mind's warning. She was too glad he was alive not to rejoice. That's all it is, she tried to tell herself. Just that. Nothing more.

Aidan took a sip of the coffee, then sighed and closed his eyes. 'Heaven,' he breathed.

'Don't say that,' Courtney said abruptly. 'You came far too close to heaven once today.'

He opened his eyes and looked at her, the green eyes serious. 'You think I'd get there, do you?'

He probably wouldn't, she realised. And she would do well to remember that. But it was difficult when he looked gentle and tired—when he had, all kidding aside, almost been eaten.

'If you behave yourself,' she retorted, but there was no animosity in it, and she avoided his eyes.

There was a long silence between them. The fire hissed and sputtered. Overhead the jungle creatures went about their business unconcerned. Courtney cradled her coffee mug in her hands and listened to the soft, reassuring rasp of Aidan's breathing.

'I'll try,' he said at last.

And for the rest of the night he did. He didn't go off to sleep right after they ate as she expected he would. On the contrary, he seemed to want company, to need to talk. And, obviously unwilling to talk about his near brush with death and not wanting to bring up her near brush with disaster that had begun the day, he steered the conversation on to non-controversial topics, mentioning Consuelo, Aurelio, and talking a bit about life in Boca Negra in general. He was entertaining, witty, and Courtney enjoyed hearing his stories.

She wondered what had brought him to the jungle in the first place, but she didn't like to ask. Not when for the first time things were going smoothly between them. Still, she did comment on some of the things he told her. And when he finished another story about how he and João had three times rebuilt a shack that kept getting ripped apart by rainstorms, she sensed once more the tenacity and commitment that was so at odds with his refusal to accept responsibility for her in the beginning.

'You like it in Boca Negra,' she commented as she repacked the cooking-gear and folded down the cover on the pack. 'And its people.'

'Yeah, I do.' He rolled into his hammock and adjusted the mosquito netting, then shut his eyes. 'Not quite your speed, I imagine.' Behind the net she couldn't distinguish his expression.

Courtney shrugged. 'A far cry from Los Angeles, that's for sure. But I was raised here, after all, and I loved growing up here.'

'So you keep saying. Why'd you leave then, if you liked it so much?'

She stopped for a minute, trying to figure out how to put an answer into words. 'To be my own person, I guess,' she said, unsure how to explain her upbringing. 'I'll be right back.' She got to her feet and retreated behind some bushes to wash her face and change her shirt. Yesterday she had gone down to the river to wash at the end of the day. But not tonight. The memory of that jaguar crouched there above Aidan's head could still make her shudder. Hurriedly she buttoned her shirt.

When she came back, she expected he would be asleep. He had looked exhausted. He had had a terrifying experience. Now he needed some time to recover. She crawled into her own hammock and lay suspended, rocking gently.

'So why *are* you back?' Aidan's question broke into the jungle sounds. 'Besides what you've already told me?'

Startled, she wasn't sure what to say. What she had told him was certainly enough. But it wasn't the whole story, and now she wasn't surprised that he had sensed it. Before tonight she wouldn't have said anything. Not anything revealing anyway. But tonight things were different. They had taken another look at each other during the last twenty-four hours. They had been tested. They had survived.

'It's a long story,' she said.

'I don't mind.' His voice was soft and sleepy. 'Tell me.'

'A bedtime story?' she teased lightly.

'Why not?' His tone turned wry. 'Unless you have a better idea of how to spend the time.'

'No,' she said quickly, but she was grateful that his frame of mind was improving. If he could start making sly innuendoes again, he was getting back to normal at least.

His laugh was dry and self-deprecating. 'I thought not.' He shifted. She could hear the rustle and creak of the hammock in the near darkness. 'So, are you going to tell me or not?'

She hadn't explained much to him before. Only that it had been imperative that she find her parents. The whys hadn't been important. But now she found herself telling him more about them, about Uncle Leander, about how she felt she needed to provide for their future.

He listened quietly, prompting her when she stopped and accepting, unlike Clarke, that she felt she had a duty to do it.

'Your parents' keeper?' Aidan's voice was quiet, almost inaudible over the sound of the tree frogs.

'Something like that.'

'Shouldn't it be the other way around?'

'Not at my age,' Courtney assured him quickly. 'I don't want them running my life.'

'Did they?'

'Oh, yes.' She swayed slightly in her own hammock, remembering.

'Most parents do.' She heard him shift slightly in his hammock. It was slung between two trees only about a foot and a half from hers. The night had gone dark and the fire still burned low, but she felt cocooned with him, enveloped in their own tiny world—just the two of them. And oddly safe.

'Not like mine,' she said.

'What do you mean?'

'Most parents cosset their children. Cherish them. Protect them.'

'Yours didn't?'

She gave a dry little laugh. 'In the long run, I suppose they did. They cared about my immortal soul. But whether or not I survived the day... well...' She tipped her head back, staring up into the darkness of the forest canopy. 'When I was little, they used to use me as a buffer between themselves and the hostile tribes we sometimes encountered.'

'What!' The sleepiness changed to outrage.

'It made sense, of course,' she told him quietly, justifying for him what she had had a hard time justifying for herself. 'It was supposed to be non-threatening to the tribe. I mean, you send a little girl in first and you show you're coming in peace, don't you?'

'Of course, but my God...' The hammock jerked as he sat up and scowled at her.

'I didn't realise it at first. I mean, I was pretty little. But when I did, later on, I got scared.'

It was the first time he had heard her sound as small and Bo-Peep-like as she had looked the first time he met her. She sounded forlorn almost. In spite of himself, he was touched. He understood, too. 'I know what you feel like, being used.'

Courtney turned her head and considered him. He had lain back down again, but he was lying now so that they faced each other. In the glow of the embers she could barely make out his face. But the seriousness of his expression was obvious, as was the sincerity of his words.

'Your parents used you, too?'

'Not my parents.' He sounded bitter. 'My wife.'

The words cut her, but she didn't speak, just waited, sensing more to come. Aidan moved restlessly, clearing his throat.

'She wasn't my wife at first, though,' he went on. 'She was a girl I knew. A girl I dated.' Another pause. 'Slept with.' The last two words came on a harsh exhalation of air.

Courtney felt a dull pain somewhere in the region of her heart. It was rather like the pain she had felt yesterday evening when she contemplated Aidan spending the night with one of the Indian women. She had forced it out of her mind then, and she tried to ignore it now. Whoever this woman was, Aidan had no fond memories of her. But she probably went a long way towards explaining just why he was the way he was.

'Her name was Shanna,' he went on in a monotone. 'She was going to Radcliffe while I was at Harvard Law.'

So he was every bit the Boston Brahmin she had thought he was.

'She was dating my room-mate, Danny. They had a falling out. She came and cried on my shoulder. I was such a sap I listened. I got infatuated, in fact. She was little, delicate——' Courtney could almost imagine the grimace in the dark '—looked a hell of a lot like you actually.'

'I won't say thanks.'

'No. It wasn't a compliment.'

'That's what I was afraid of.'

'But at the time I thought she was great. I didn't know why Danny disagreed, but I was glad he did. I wanted her for myself. And she seemed to want me.' There was a long pause. 'What she wanted was my money.'

'You were rich?' It wasn't as incongruous as it sounded on first hearing. She could imagine Aidan Sawyer in pinstripes and rep ties, starched shirts and cufflinks. Harvard Law might be a million light years from what he was doing now, but Courtney was willing to bet it took the same toughness to get through it.

'My dad was. Is,' he corrected. He sighed and rolled on to his back, folding his arms behind his head. 'And so is Shanna now.'

'What happened?'

His mouth twisted in a bitter smile. 'The standard. We slept together. She said she was pregnant. She didn't just tell me. She made a point of telling my parents, too. Announced it at the family Sunday dinner. The only time I've ever seen my mother at a loss for words. But not for long.'

'No?'

'No. The edict came down from on high that very afternoon. Sons of Ethan Sawyer did not have bastard children. I had a responsibility to Shanna. To my unborn child.' He said the word *responsibility* exactly the way he had said it when he had told her he wouldn't take responsibility for her. There was a better than even bet the two were related, she thought. Imagine that.

'What happened?' she asked him softly.

'What do you think?' His voice was harsh. 'I was expected to do "the right thing" and marry her.'

'They forced you?'

She felt more than saw him shrug. 'You couldn't really call it that. At the time I didn't care. I guess I thought I loved her. And she seemed to be just the right sort of ornament for a Boston lawyer to have on his arm. So we got married.'

Something large, a tapir perhaps, crashed through the brush not far away. But for once Courtney hardly noticed. Her attention was entirely on the man lying in the hammock next to hers. 'It didn't work out?' she ventured finally.

'No.'

She was half-way afraid he was going to say that and nothing more. She could feel him struggling, could taste his bitterness, and wanted to share it.

Finally he spoke again. His voice was hard-edged, cutting. 'She wasn't even pregnant. She had——' and here the bitterness dripped from his voice '—"made a mistake", she said. There was no mistake. She wanted a rich husband and I was the sucker she chose. And the hell of it is, I was too dumb even then to toss her out on her ear. I had been brought up on that "marriage is for ever" crap. I thought we'd just make the best of it. I never told my parents what she had done. And she just said it was a miscarriage. They always thought she was a saint.' He snorted. 'Then she really did get pregnant.'

Courtney held her breath. She heard Aidan suck in his. His whole body seemed clenched, radiating tension. She wanted to reach out, to touch him, to give him release.

'She had an abortion.' The bitterness turned to momentary anguish. Then, as abruptly as it had entered his voice, it vanished and he said dully, 'She didn't want children, she said. She only wanted the good life, wealth and whatever it could provide. She just used me to get it. I left her then. I packed it in and left them all.'

'That's when you came to Boca Negra?' Courtney asked him softly.

'That's when,' Aidan confirmed. 'To be my own man. Not tied down by anyone. Not to be used. No more traps for me. Never again.'

CHAPTER SIX

COURTNEY understood his feelings better than he could have imagined.

Two of a kind, we are, she told herself as she drifted off to sleep at last. She felt an uncanny empathy towards Aidan Sawyer. Two of a kind.

But the next morning she changed her mind.

When she awakened, he was already up and stomping around, being his normal irascible, obnoxious self. At first he grumbled about how long it took her to comb her hair and then he asked the heavens again why he had ever let her manipulate him into doing this anyway. The man who had shared his painful past with her just hours before might never have existed at all. She couldn't figure him out.

'Hurry up,' he growled at her when she was still trying to untangle her damp hair.

'I am hurrying,' she assured him calmly, still hoping to see a return of the man she had discovered in him last night. 'What's wrong? Do you think there are hostile Indians on our tail still? Or another jaguar?'

'Who knows?' Aidan said darkly, hands on hips. He glared at her as if everything wrong in the world were her fault. 'Indians, miners, jaguars and God knows what else.'

Courtney frowned. 'Do you really think the tribe would get angry because we left? Would that man who...who...' She couldn't quite get the words out. 'Would he say?'

'Not likely.' Aidan dismissed the idea. 'I suspect he wouldn't want it generally known that he'd tried and failed—especially given the chief's "respect" for you.'

Courtney threw her comb at him. 'Rat.'

'Impatient rat,' he agreed, tossing the comb back. 'Get a move on. We've got plenty of ground to cover today. Since we did leave without an explanation, I would just as soon not be anywhere close enough for them to stumble on.' So saying, he turned on his heel and headed for the boat.

Courtney stared after him, unsure what to make of his behaviour.

'Come *on*,' she heard him holler again a few moments later. So, gathering up her gear, she went after him.

His mood didn't improve substantially during the course of the morning. He didn't say much beyond the odd comment about a bit of flora or fauna they were passing. A personal remark never crossed his lips. She found herself feeling slightly bereft, then told herself that was nonsense. She ought to be grateful for small favours. Crabby though he was, he didn't go out of his way to annoy her quite as much as he had. And he didn't seem to delight in criticising her as thoroughly either. At least not with the same bitter edge to his words that she had felt so often before. So perhaps the sense of peace that she had felt between them briefly last night wasn't totally a product of her imagination.

She didn't spend much time dwelling on it, anyway, because some time after they stopped for lunch, they ran into a lone Indian who didn't vanish into the forest the moment they laid eyes on him. Courtney felt a stab of fear, but Aidan shook his head.

'Not the same tribe,' he told her in an undertone, then cut the engine and called out to him. The man pointed at Courtney, shouting something back.

Aidan's eyes widened. 'He knows who you are.'

Courtney stared. 'He said . . .?'

'He said, 'Is that the missionaries' daughter?''

Courtney shook her head, disbelieving. It didn't make sense. But if Aidan said it, it must be true. He wouldn't have any reason to lie about it. 'Does he know my parents?'

Aidan shouted the question at the man on the bank. His answering nod was obvious to both of them, but just to make sure Aidan turned to her and said, 'It won't be long now.'

She swivelled around to look at him. 'What do you mean?'

'He's a member of the tribe where your parents are living.'

'Are they...' She felt a moment of panic. Unspeakable thoughts that she had refused to acknowledge before surfaced now and wouldn't be denied. If he knew her, perhaps he was looking for her. Perhaps something really had happened to them that had prevented them from writing. 'They *are* all right, aren't they?'

'They're fine,' Aidan assured her. 'Hale and hearty, I would guess. At least he didn't say they weren't.'

'What did he say?'

'That we ought to reach them before sundown.' He squinted at his watch. 'About three hours or less, by my estimation.'

Courtney swallowed hard, then licked her lips which felt suddenly dry even in the Amazonian humidity.

'And that they're expecting you.'

Her jaw dropped. 'How could they be?'

Aidan shrugged. 'Who knows? That's what he said, though.'

Courtney frowned. Expecting her? Missing her, perhaps? The possibility intrigued her. A smile began to play at the corners of her mouth. Perhaps they really did miss her. Perhaps they were talking about her, hoping she would turn up to visit them. The smile grew broader for a moment, then uncertainty crept in and the smile faded.

Aidan tipped his head to one side and considered her like a doctor diagnosing a patient. 'Nervous?' he asked. 'Feeling a bit like the prodigal daughter?'

Courtney shrugged. 'I haven't squandered the family fortune at least.'

'No. They're going to do that themselves if you don't stop them, aren't they?'

She nodded reluctantly. 'It could happen.'

'You won't let it.'

'No.'

'But they might kill the fatted calf for you just the same,' he said encouragingly.

She wouldn't have bet on it. But the Indian had said they were expecting her. And now he had disappeared into the forest again, most likely headed towards the village to share the news of her arrival. So maybe . . . just maybe . . . they would. Where her parents were concerned she could rarely predict what they would do.

'Would yours?' she asked Aiden. 'If you went home?'

'I'm not going home,' he said bluntly. 'Ever.' And he cut in the engine again, drowning out any further conversation, letting her know in no uncertain terms that what he had said last night was not to be discussed again.

'Did you tell them you were coming?' he asked her later, obviously dwelling on the question of her being expected as much as she was.

'I wrote them letters,' she replied. 'Tons of letters. All about Uncle Leander and all that.'

'But they didn't answer?'

She shook her head. 'No. And I never wrote and said I was coming. I didn't take the time.'

'Strange,' Aiden commented.

'Yes.' Courtney agreed with that. It didn't make sense. At least then it didn't.

It began to early that evening as they rounded a bend in the river and heard a shout. A small Indian boy jumped up and down, waved, then turned and ran off into the jungle as quick as his legs would carry him. Moments later he reappeared, followed by three Indian women, an Indian man, and a white woman.

'Mother!'

Marguerite Perkins was a sprightly woman with hair now grey that had once been as blonde as her daughter's. She wore it long and coiled up on top of her head in a braid and it made her look like a schoolgirl. And she sounded as eager as a schoolgirl on the first day of summer holidays when she called, 'You came!' and ran to meet her daughter at the water's edge. 'Daddy said you would!' she added triumphantly.

Courtney was perplexed. '*Daddy* said...?' But she didn't have a chance to finish the sentence because her mother was hauling her out of the boat and into her arms, wrapping her in a hug that was surprisingly strong for such a bird-like woman. Then she held her daughter out at arm's length and smiled.

'Just look at you. Such a beauty! Rob will be so pleased.'

'Who's Rob?' Courtney asked, her confusion growing.

But her mother hooked her arm through her daughter's, then glanced over her shoulder at Aidan, still in the boat. 'Come along now, you too,' she said to him. Then turning once more to her daughter she continued, 'Oh, I'm just so glad you finally got here!'

'Mother, I——' But Courtney's protests went unheeded. Marguerite had a firm grip on her hand and was hauling her along a narrow path inland from the river. She had no real choice but to allow herself to be hauled, managing only to spare a backward glance at Aidan who gave her a grin and mouthed, 'The fatted calf?'

She gave him a bewildered look in return. It certainly sounded like it. How unusual. The only other times she could remember arriving in the village where her parents were living, when she was young enough to have still been away at school, they had scarcely seemed to notice her return. Things were, perhaps, looking up.

But she still wanted to know who this Rob her mother had referred to was. And would he care if she were a 'beauty' or not? She gazed around curiously as she was tugged along on the monologue of her mother's enthusiasm.

The village wasn't much different from the one she and Aidan had stolen out of in the middle of the night the day before. It was like enough, in fact, for Courtney to glance around with a touch of apprehension, wary of anyone who might deign to smile at her or, worse, wink. But it seemed everyone was smiling, chattering, laughing. They were all obviously enormously pleased to see her.

'I wondered if you'd come,' Marguerite said to her as she led Courtney through the closest hut and out into the round in the centre of the village. 'I thought you might not. Or I thought you might not get the letter.'

'What letter? I *didn't* get any letter,' Courtney said. 'That's why I'm here. Because of Uncle Leander.'

'Uncle Leander?' Her mother sounded totally baffled. 'We didn't write you about Leander. You never got our letter?'

'Never. I haven't heard a word out of you for over a year. And you know about the trust. Uncle Leander is ready to get the lawyers to try to break it, and I had to stop him. So I came. I came to prove to him that you were really still alive—that some day you'd be home and need that money.'

But as she spoke, her mother began to smile and shake her head. Her confusion had obviously cleared, and now she patted Courtney's hand as if to humour her.

'That's what *you* think,' she said when Courtney stopped speaking.

'What?'

'You really came to marry Robert.'

Surely she was hearing things. Surely her mother hadn't just said something about marrying someone. Heavens above, she didn't even *know* anyone named Robert!

'Mother, I'm here because of Leander. I need to get Daddy to write and sign a letter giving his whereabouts, I need to have it witnessed, and I need to get back to Los Angeles within three weeks.'

But Marguerite had more important things on her mind. She was shaking her head and murmuring about how Courtney was getting more lovely with every passing year and how pleased Robert would be, and how right Endicott had been to think of it.

'Mother,' Courtney tried again. But her words were cut off at once by a booming voice.

'Ah, daughter!' And she was quite suddenly enveloped in a fatherly hug. 'At last!'

Endicott Perkins beamed down at her, still as burly and beneficent as ever, his snowy white hair and wire-rimmed glasses making him look positively cherubic. He looked, too, as if he had just pulled off a minor miracle, and if he actually thought she was going to marry someone called Robert on his say-so, she supposed he might imagine that he had.

'Dad,' she said, giving him an awkward hug in return. But all the time she was hugging him, her eyes were busy darting around the sea of faces, all of them darkly bronzed and smiling, none of them looking as if they might belong to someone called Robert.

'I knew you'd come when you got the letter,' he told her, looping his arm over her shoulder and hugging her against him while he towed her into what was most likely his hut. She glanced around and was grateful for once to see Aidan following her, even if he did have a bemused look on his face.

'I didn't get any letter, Dad,' she protested again.

'No?' He looked momentarily amazed, then beamed even more broadly than before. 'An act of the Spirit, then,' he pronounced it.

Courtney gulped. She had no doubt that the Spirit was active in the world. She just didn't want anyone, least of all her father, thinking that her arrival here had owed anything to It.

She started to tell him about Uncle Leander, but he scarcely paid attention. 'Leander's an old tightwad, quite probably in league with the devil,' he informed her. Then he chuckled. 'How deliciously ironic. To think of Leander unwittingly being a messenger of good.'

'I don't think——' Courtney began, but her father cut her off.

'It's not really important. The important thing,' he told Courtney expansively, 'is that Robert needs a bride and here you are! An answer to our prayers.'

'And our letter as well, even if you didn't get it,' Marguerite added, smiling at her daughter.

Courtney tried to smile in return, while her mind was frantically winging all over the place. 'Who's Robert?' She still couldn't see anyone she thought might possibly be him.

Endicott laughed. 'My assistant pastor, I think you'd say—if I had a regular church. He's another missionary.'

'A lovely young man,' Marguerite chimed in. 'Right out of Yale Divinity. From a long line of holy men. So sincere. So kind. So devout. So handsome.'

'And a bachelor,' Endicott added, as if Courtney hadn't figured that out already.

'It's his one drawback,' her mother continued. It sounded as if they had rehearsed it. If Courtney didn't know them so well, she might have expected that they had. But she knew they simply thought with one mind. And now they thought she ought to marry whoever this Robert was.

God, they hadn't changed a bit. They'd just gone from offering her to Indian tribes to offering her to unknown men!

'Harder for single men to be effective here,' her father was saying as he bustled her into the centre of the village. 'The people like to see stability if you're living with them. They don't like to think you might be...' he coughed delicately '...interested in their women.' His normally ruddy cheeks got a bit ruddier.

'We told Robert that he really needs a wife,' Marguerite said brightly. 'We told him all about you.'

'And he wants to marry me?' Courtney asked hollowly.

'Thinks it's a capital idea,' Endicott said jovially. 'He sees the wisdom of it.'

'Oh, of course.' He would. Probably thought it was part of his vocation. She thought she might faint. Except if she did, chances were when she came to she would be married. She wasn't about to take the risk.

'Dad,' she tried gamefully. 'I didn't get your letter. I didn't know anything about this.'

'What difference does that make?' both of her parents chorused, the first signs of worry creasing their seraphic faces.

'Well, I——'

'You're needed here. Needed to do the Lord's work. Needed to be Robert's wife.'

The primeval panic was upon her, the age-old fear of being thrust into the breach once again. 'That's...that's why I came actually,' she babbled, groping her way as she spoke. 'Besides Uncle Leander, I mean. I came to...' she floundered '...to tell you that I...I'm already getting married.' She couldn't very well marry their Robert if she was already engaged, could she?

'Married?' Marguerite's face fell.

'Married? You?' Consternation turned Endicott's features to a worried frown. 'Married?' he repeated, as if it would disappear if they said it three times.

The group of Indians who had been standing witness to the entire proceeding seemed to have caught that one word at least. They began murmuring among themselves, the word being repeated in English, in Portuguese, in whatever language they spoke.

'Yes, married,' Courtney confirmed, casting about frantically for something to back the lie up with.

'To whom?' her father demanded.

She opened her mouth and willed her brain to come up with an answer. Any answer.

'To me,' Aidan Sawyer said.

CHAPTER SEVEN

COURTNEY thought she must have gone through the looking glass with Alice. A fitting punishment probably, considering the lie she had just told. But had Aidan Sawyer really just compounded it tenfold by saying, 'To me'?

She spun and stared at him. He was standing just behind her, that slightly mocking half-smile on his face as he looked from one dumbfounded parent to another. Then the smile tipped a little more generously on the left side and he nodded his head in confirmation at the same time that he laid a proprietorial hand on his new fiancée's shoulder.

'And you are...?' her father demanded, scrutinising this stranger who was so inopportunely spoiling his plans.

Aidan looked down at Courtney, obviously waiting to be properly introduced. He gave her an encouraging wink. She looked away quickly. Winks made her more than a bit nervous these days. And she was having trouble finding her voice.

'This, uh, this is...Aidan Sawyer, Dad,' she managed at last. She turned to Aidan and said rather helplessly because it was all too obvious, 'I'd like you to meet my mother and father.'

'I'm pleased to meet you, sir.' Aidan stuck out his hand, which the Reverend considered for a split second before deciding that it was his Christian duty to shake it. 'I've heard a lot about you.'

'Well, we've heard absolutely nothing about you, Mr Sawyer,' Marguerite said bluntly. 'Honestly, Courtney,' she scolded her daughter. 'How could you not have written? How could you not have said?'

'It...it...I...'

'It happened fast, Mrs Perkins,' Aidan told her in his nasal Boston drawl. 'You know the feeling...love at first sight and, well, I took one look at Courtney and...' he grinned '...she knocked me off my feet!'

Courtney choked, then glared at Aidan. He stared back in wide-eyed innocence.

'Well, I...' For a moment Marguerite seemed just as at sea as her daughter was. Then she allowed, 'Well, yes, I guess I do know,' and she looked adoringly into Endicott's eyes and gave her husband's arm a hearty squeeze. 'It must have been just like Chippy and I were.'

Courtney wanted to laugh at the thought of her mother and father having a relationship even remotely similar to hers and Aidan Sawyer's. How could anyone actually believe she was going to marry him?

But what alternative did she have? Was she going to open her mouth now and say it had all been a joke? A pretty tasteless one at that? And if she did, what then?

She would probably end up marrying Robert, that's what.

So she mustered up an adoring smile of her own and bestowed it on Aidan. 'I didn't know what hit me,' she said, which was certainly the truth. 'And, er, I...wanted to surprise you.'

'But Robert...' Her father tried one last time. 'He...I told him...I promised...I...' He looked bewildered, as if God had changed sides half-way through the game.

'I'm sure he'll understand,' Aidan said easily. 'And,' he added with just the right amount of forcefulness, 'I wouldn't, if you persuaded Courtney it was her duty to marry him and jilt me.'

One look at Aidan's hard face and Endicott Perkins shook his head rapidly. 'No, no, dear boy. Wouldn't think of it.'

'Good.' Aidan gave him a bland smile that belied his words. He would have had a great future in the courtroom, Courtney thought. He could intimidate with the best of them. The world of criminal justice had no idea what it had lost.

'Now,' Aidan was saying, 'I think Courtney could use a bit of a rest before she catches you up on any more of her news and hears any more of yours. We both could.'

Courtney hoped this wasn't yet another ploy to share her hammock. But she didn't have time to give it more than a passing thought because Marguerite took him up on his hint at once. 'Of course, dear, come with me.'

Marguerite led her daughter to the hut that Endicott had come out of earlier, and pointed out a partitioned area that already had a hammock slung in it. 'We've been ready for you.'

Courtney smiled. 'How nice.'

Somewhere deep down she wished it had been for all the normal parental reasons that most mothers and fathers were eager to see their children again. But chances were that wasn't ever going to happen. She supposed she ought to be grateful they even remembered she existed. On the other hand, if they hadn't she wouldn't be in the mess she was in now.

'I'll just bring the rest of her gear in.' Aidan was following them, a duffel bag gripped in each hand.

Marguerite gave him a flustered smile. 'Oh yes, do. Thank you so much.' She gave him another wary look, rather like a mother who, having sent her daughter to the pet store to buy a kitten, discovers that the girl has brought home a tiger instead. 'We can accommodate you, too, I'm sure, Mr Sawyer. You're not...not...' She looked helplessly from her daughter to Aidan, her cheeks reddening at her thoughts.

'No, Mother, we're not,' Courtney said firmly. 'Thank you for helping me get settled. If you don't mind, I would like to rest now.' And get my bearings, she added silently, try to see what I can salvage from the chaos of my life.

Marguerite patted her arm. 'That's just fine, dear. And after you do, perhaps you can...can meet Robert.' Even as she said the words, the fact that meeting Robert was not going to have the significance they had hoped seemed to be borne in on her. She looked very tired. 'You rest, dear,' she counselled. 'And now, Mr Sawyer...'

'He'll be along in a minute, Mother.' Courtney wasn't letting him get away without a word. If nothing else she was going to banish that dreadful smirk from his face.

'Whatever you like, darling.' Marguerite fluttered her hands helplessly, then dashed out of the hut.

'How could you?' Courtney whirled on him, sparks flying.

'How could I not?' Aidan countered, infuriating her further. 'Did you want to marry old holier-than-thou Robert?'

'Of course not!'

'Then who were you going to suggest marrying?' he wanted to know. He leaned against one of the heavy wooden supports and folded his arms across his chest, waiting for an answer.

She couldn't think of a soul. Clarke? Hardly. He would have been no match for her parents in person, let alone thousands of miles away. If she had mentioned Clarke, they would have talked her out of it before she had said a hundred words. Besides, they would know instinctively that she wouldn't come by herself to announce her engagement. They would expect her to bring her fiancé with her. And God help her, she *had* brought Aidan.

'I don't know,' she snapped. She hugged her arms tightly against her chest, pacing the dirt floor of the hut, fuming, feeling trapped. 'I would have thought of something,' she lied.

'Sure you would have,' he scoffed.

She glowered at him. He smiled.

'By the way,' he added off-handedly, a hint of a grin hovering at the corner of his mouth, 'what is it we're not?'

'What?'

'Your mother said, ''You're not...'' and you said, ''No, Mother, we're not.'' Not what?'

'Aidan!'

Wide-eyed innocence mocked her. 'Not what?' he repeated.

'Sleeping together!'

'Ah!'

She was blushing furiously. 'You knew damned well what she was asking.'

He gave her a smug grin. 'Just wanted to be certain.'

'Well, we aren't!'

'I know that.' His whole demeanour changed suddenly. He looked and sounded grave now, all the mocking gone. 'Do you want to tell them I was kidding? Do you want to beg off?'

She blinked, confused.

'We can,' he told her quietly.

'I—I don't know.' Her mind whirled with possibilities, none of them palatable. She sighed and ran her hands through her hair. 'No,' she said at last. 'No, I guess not.' She sighed. 'Because unfortunately, you're the only fiancé they would believe.'

She scowled at the doorway through which she heard her father directing someone to do something. She felt a sudden surge of anger. Why the hell couldn't he for once just have been glad to see her without trying to direct her life, too?

'Right,' Aidan said then. 'So for the moment we're engaged.'

The words had a startling effect on her. The physical reaction that she had had to him the first moment she saw him—the sense that this man was more attractive than any man had a right to be—brought her head up with a jerk.

Engaged to Aidan Sawyer? A frisson of desire shivered down her spine, followed by a moment of pure panic. 'Purely a sham,' she said defensively.

He gave her a hard look. 'You're damned right about that.'

Well, that was putting her in her place. Certainly she wasn't expecting anything different, was she? Heavens, no. She gave him a brisk nod, accepting his words, hoping actually that he would leave. A rest sounded like just the thing—one from which she might wake up and discover this was all a bad dream.

But Aidan didn't move. He stood waiting, regarding her with that faint, amused smile on his face.

'Well?' she snarled.

'Give us a kiss, sweetheart?' he drawled.

She heaved her duffel bag at him. He dodged it, grinning.

By the time her mother came to get her for the evening meal, she thought she could cope. She hoped so, at least. After all, it only required being civil to Aidan until they left again. She would visit a few days, then excuse herself by saying that Aidan had to get back to work. They would leave, and that would be that. She followed her mother out of the hut, smiling, able to face the situation with some equanimity at last.

She was momentarily taken aback though, when her father swooped down on her, a cookie-jar-shaped blond man in tow. 'This is Robert,' he announced, hauling the round young man forward—as if he needed an introduction.

'I'm pleased to meet you,' Courtney said, shaking his hand, thinking that he looked holier than she did right off the bat. Aidan seemed to be thinking the same thing if the look on his face was anything to judge by. 'I've just been hearing good things about you from my parents.'

Robert blushed. She could have predicted it. 'And I've heard good things about you, too,' he told her sincerely.

She would have bet on that. 'Well, I don't suppose you heard I'm getting married,' she said.

Robert's jaw dropped.

'To me,' Aidan added.

Courtney shot him a baleful look over her shoulder. He was getting into a rut, saying the same thing over and over. When his hand came down on her shoulder like a vice, it was all she could do not to flinch.

'Aren't you going to introduce us, darling?'

She stepped backward and ground her sandal on his toes. His fingers resumed strangling her shoulder. 'Robert, I'd like you to meet my...fiancé...Aidan Sawyer.'

'I—I'm...pleased to—to meet you,' Robert gulped.

'Likewise.'

The two men shook hands, Aidan with a determination in his grip that was obvious to all present. Courtney desperately wanted to poke him in the ribs and tell him it wasn't arm-wrestling he was engaged in. She contented herself by merely stepping between them, when Robert seemed to go slightly white around the mouth, and saying brightly, 'Mother tells me you went to Yale, Bob.'

'Robert,' he corrected automatically, then blushed an even more vivid red. 'Er, yes...I...I did.' He got his hand loose from Aidan's and was cautiously rubbing the feeling back into it with his left one.

'How long have you been down here?' Courtney asked politely.

'Six months.'

'And do you like it?'

'Oh, yes.' His eyes lit up at last. 'It's my life's work. It's what I've always wanted...bringing enlightenment to...'

He went on at length, but she stopped listening after enlightenment. Robert was her father reincarnate. The same zeal, the same intensity, the same single-minded fervour that saw the rest of life as second in importance. She plastered an attentive smile on her face, pretending to be listening. But in fact she could have been a million miles away. And she knew she would never have married him in a million years.

She didn't think anyone noticed her inattention really—not until later that evening after dinner when her parents finally gave her a break, allowing her to escape down to the river where she sat on a log on the bank and stared off towards where it disappeared around a bend.

She had vanished without a word, needing space, and was sitting quietly, trying to get a perspective on the events of the day, trying to sort out what to do next, when she heard a twig break behind her. She started, turning abruptly.

'Oh, it's you.'

Adian came out of the shadows and stood looking down at her, unnerving her. She cracked her knuckles and tried to ignore him. 'Not a very enthusiastic welcome for your new fiancé.' He was grinning at her.

Her lips pressed together in a thin line. 'My sham fiancé,' she reminded him stiffly.

He squatted down next to her. Her eyes dropped, but she could still see the way the faded denim fabric pulled tautly over the muscles of his thighs. He was scant inches from her, and she felt an almost overwhelming desire to reach out and touch the soft cloth, to run her finger over the top of his knee, up the seam of his jeans. She swallowed, licking her suddenly dry lips. Her heart pounded.

'Sham fiancé,' he concurred, his mouth twisting slightly as he said it.

She scowled at him. 'What are you doing here, anyway? What do you want?'

'I came looking for you.'

Her scowl deepened. 'Why?'

One eyebrow lifted derisively. 'Because I'm your fiancé?'

She grimaced. 'You didn't have to come looking for me.'

He shoved a hand through his hair in an irritated way. 'I damned well did.'

'Why?'

'Don't be obtuse. Because I'm your fiancé,' he said tightly, 'and your parents expect me to. For God's sake, you wander off into the jungle by yourself, leaving the man you're supposed to be marrying behind! What the hell was I supposed to do?'

'Stay there!'

He shook his head adamantly. 'No, thanks. Besides, if I hadn't come, your father would have sent Robert.'

'He wouldn't.'

'He sure as hell would. You might be out of sight, out of mind when you're a few thousand miles away. But when you're in his neighbourhood, he's concerned about you. You're his daughter, for heaven's sake. And I don't like the way he looks at me,' Aidan grumbled.

'How does he look at you?' Courtney was curious.

'Like I'm some sort of lecher.' Aidan's voice was a growl.

'Perhaps he's clairvoyant.'

It was Aidan's turn to scowl. 'Fat lot of leching I've done.'

'Not for want of trying.'

He shifted uncomfortably. Had she embarrassed him, God forbid? Courtney grinned. Aidan glanced over his shoulder, frowned a moment, then changed his position, kneeling instead of simply squatting, moving in on her. And before she knew what he was about, he was sliding his arms around her and drawing her into his arms.

'Wh——' But the rest of the word was smothered by his mouth covering hers, his lips tasting hers, persuading her, melting her. Heavens!

He had caught her off balance and she began to slip sideways off the log. His arms tightened around her, pulling her back, drawing her off the log and on to his lap. For a moment, her legs scrambled frantically, her arms flailed, and then her hormones took over.

The kiss changed, too, softening, deepening. For such a hard man, his mouth seemed unbelievably soft, his tongue gentle as it skated lightly along the inner edge of her lips, teasing them, touching her teeth, seeking entry.

Shivering, Courtney let him in.

She couldn't do otherwise. For if she tried to recall the man who mocked her, the man who teased her, the man who had literally knocked her off her feet and right into the river, she also remembered the man who had saved her from being attacked, the man who had allowed himself to be blackmailed into helping her find her parents, who had listened to her miseries last night and had shared miseries of his own.

Her hands smoothed over the muscles of his back, then crept up to tangle in the dark thickness of his hair. He groaned softly when he felt her respond. Then all at once he was setting her aside and wiping his hand across the back of his mouth.

Courtney, having been abruptly deposited back on the log where she had started, stared at him, heart hammering, lips tingling, mind spinning. 'Wh——' she began again.

'Staking my claim,' Aidan said roughly. He glanced over his shoulder in the direction of the village. 'Robert was back there.'

'Robert?' She could scarcely get a hold on the word. 'You did *that* because of Robert?' Humiliation was fast overtaking passion. She pressed her fist against her mouth.

Aidan shrugged. 'Why not?' His mouth twisted into a wry grimace. 'It's only what he'd expect.'

Courtney averted her eyes. Only what he'd expect. Damn it all anyway. She gritted her teeth. And she, stupid fool that she was, had responded! Oh, you idiot! she chastised herself. She got jerkily to her feet and glared down at him. 'Well, thank you very much for your prompt assistance, Mr Sawyer. Just don't think it's going to get you any more than that.'

And without waiting to see if he answered her or not, she plunged down the narrow path that led back to the village. She brushed past her parents and flung herself into her hammock without even saying goodnight. She couldn't. She couldn't face anyone. At least not until morning.

* * *

In the morning her mother tried one last-ditch effort to get her to reconsider.

'How much do you know about your Mr Sawyer, darling?' she asked Courtney as they scrubbed clothes together on the side of the river.

Courtney bent her head over the shirt she was rubbing on the rocks. 'Enough.' And that was the truth and nothing but. The memory of his kiss had kept her awake for hours. Long after she had heard him say goodnight to her parents and go off to whatever hut they had put him in, long after everyone else had turned in, she had lain there and stared at the thatched roof above her head and had tried to make sense of what she had felt.

The kiss had jolted her. She had never experienced one like it before. Oh, Clarke had kissed her. He had done plenty of pawing and petting, if the truth were known. But whatever he had done, Courtney had remained detached. She had felt almost as if she were an outside observer, watching the proceedings, curious but not intimately involved.

She had been intimately involved this time. There wasn't any doubt about that. And Aidan had played her for a fool. Just putting on a show for Robert! Her cheeks had burned for hours.

They were burning now when she remembered it, though she was fairly certain her mother would only think it was from the exertion with which she was scrubbing the shirt.

'He seems . . . well . . . scruffy . . .' Marguerite ventured.

'We've been travelling, Mom.'

'Yes, but . . . he's . . . he's . . . so . . . tough.'

And that was putting it mildly, Courtney thought. She could well imagine that Aidan Sawyer wasn't the sort to please her mother. Her mother would like the heart-on-the-sleeve sort that her father was. The mild, tolerant-to-the-point-of-condescending sort of man that undoubtedly Robert was. She doubted that Robert would ever have knocked anyone unconscious the way Aidan had when he had rescued her. She also doubted that Robert would have knocked her in the river.

'He's lived in a tough world,' she said.

'So have we, but we aren't so...'

'Hard?'

'Well, yes,' Marguerite admitted. 'Are you sure, dear? It seems to me that Robert—or someone like him——' she amended quickly so that it wouldn't seem as blatant as it really was '—would be so much more *suitable*. For everything.'

'Not,' Courtney said firmly, 'for me.'

But regardless of how unsuitable Robert was for her, she still didn't like having to lie to her parents. It bothered her. Made her irritable. It didn't help that right after she had that conversation with her mother, she had an almost identical and far less satisfactory one with her father.

'What do you know about him?' Endicott demanded when she sought shelter from the midday sun in one of the huts and found him in there writing his sermon.

'I know I love him,' Courtney said, crossing her fingers behind her back.

'And you think that's enough?'

'Yes.'

Her father sighed. 'But what good is he? What good does he do?'

A powerful lot of good, Courtney thought to herself. He saved me from being raped. He got me to you so you won't lose your blasted inheritance. 'He helps people, Dad,' she said, not wanting to be more specific than that.

Her father looked sceptical. 'How?'

She told him about João's hut that Aidan had rebuilt time and again. She mentioned his willingness to help her find her parents. She didn't mention the coercion involved. And she definitely didn't mention his saving her from disaster two nights earlier. But she said enough to quell that argument. At least for the time being.

'I don't know what you see in him, though,' her father lamented.

Neither do I, Courtney thought. But there was something, whether she liked it or not. Not that it would do her any good, of course. And thinking that, her irritation grew all over again.

It got worse actually whenever she was around Aidan for any length of time. It made her testy and short with him, and she saw her parents giving her curious looks.

'You're going to have a hard time convincing them you really love me,' Aidan told her finally the next afternoon, 'if you keep giving me those dirty looks.'

'Sorry.' Her voice was purposely cool. 'I didn't know it was that obvious.'

'Only if you have eyes.'

Courtney's eyes narrowed.

He grinned. 'You're doing it again.'

She made a truly awful face and he laughed at her. 'Come on,' he said. 'Walk with me.'

She looked at him suspiciously. 'Where?'

'Down to the river.'

'What if Robert follows us?'

'You mean, will I kiss you again?'

She might have known he would be that blunt. 'I just want you to know it isn't necessary,' she told him gruffly.

'A matter of opinion.'

'Well, my opinion is that it's absolutely not necessary.'

'I thought it was fun.'

Fun was not the word she would have used. But she had no desire to correct him. 'I'll only go if you...if you...behave.'

That made him laugh. 'I'll be a regular Jane Austen hero, sweetheart. Come on.'

She didn't have much choice actually. Her father was heading her way, Robert in tow, and she knew as sure as anything that he had something up his sleeve. Her father never did anything without a purpose. And while her mother had seemed almost reconciled to her marriage, she didn't think her father had entirely given up making the world in his own image. Probably by now he had thought of some more reasons that she and Robert were suited for each other despite her engagement to Aidan.

She allowed Aidan to take her by the arm and lead her away. He didn't speak until they had left her father and Robert far behind them. Nor, unfortunately, did he let go of her arm. Even when they reached the river-bank, he kept his fingers firmly around her wrist, and she felt as if all the nerve-endings in her whole arm were centred in the few inches where his callused fingers gripped her smooth skin.

She tripped over a root and stumbled. Aidan's arm went around her, hauling her upright against the hard wall of his ribs at the same time.

'I'm all right,' she said hastily, pulling away.

'Are you?' He allowed her a few inches breathing space—not enough. Never enough. And she looked at him suspiciously, trying to discern mockery in his tone. Oddly enough, there didn't seem to be any. He was looking at her with something akin to concern. She found it totally unnerving.

'Well, of course, I am,' she said briskly, 'what did you think? I only tripped.'

'I didn't mean about that. I meant, are things all right with your parents and you?'

'Of course they are.'

He looked unconvinced. 'You mean they're like this all the time?'

'Like what?'

'Managing. Bossy. Father knows best.'

She shrugged unhappily. 'I'm afraid so.'

'Are they making things hard for you?'

'About what?'

He gave her a pained look. 'Don't be coy. You know damned well what. Robert. And you. And me.'

Courtney sighed and leaned back against a tree trunk. 'I think they're coming to terms with it. I mean, my mother has...uh, questioned my sanity about getting involved with you, but...' She smiled and shook her head.

Aidan scowled. 'What's wrong with me?'

Courtney rolled her eyes. 'How can I tell thee? Let me count the ways.'

'I'm saving your hide, sweetheart,' he reminded her without qualms.

'I keep telling myself that,' she said gruffly.

He gave her an offended look. 'So much for gratitude.' And without another word, he spun on his heel and stalked off into the forest.

Courtney stared after him, baffled. What was eating him? One minute he was propositioning her, the next he was oh-so-sincere and almost avuncular, then he was teasing, then serious, then offended, then... Men! Would she never figure them out?

She considered going after Aidan, then thought about walking back to the village, and finally decided to stay right where she was. A little peace and quiet might be just what she needed right now.

It didn't last long. As she was sitting quietly in the crook of a tree, watching a family of capybaras on the opposite bank, she heard a great rustling and thumping close at hand. Aidan never made that much noise, nor did any Indian she had ever met. Only tapirs—she felt a stab of panic—and her father.

'Ah, there you are!' He peered up into the tree at her, a satisfied smile on his face. 'Hoped I'd find you.' He came closer and said confidentially, 'Hoped I'd find you without what's-his-name.'

'Aidan,' Courtney said stiffly.

'Yes, yes. Just so.' He settled down on a log just below her and patted the spot beside him. 'Plenty of room for two down here.'

Courtney warily looked at the spot he indicated. She remembered other logs, other spots. Other father-daughter chats. She remembered when she was not more than five and her father had sat her down and explained how he was going to let her be the leader in a follow-my-leader game. How he was going to let her be the leader and go into the next village first. She remembered how she had thought it was a great honour. She remembered another chat when she was twelve, when he had told her how lucky she was going to be to go to the convent school in Belém. And another when she was fifteen and he had told her how she would love California at that time of year. She wondered what he thought she would love this time. Robert probably.

She wasn't far wrong.

When she finally did lower herself from the branch and came to sit on the log with him, albeit a couple of feet away, her father stared out over the river and began to tell her about the work he had been doing since she had been gone. It was a long, roundabout dissertation of his accomplishments—and they were many and impressive—and Courtney was almost lulled into thinking that his comments would have nothing to do with her. And then, all of a sudden, they came home to roost.

'But I'm getting old,' he said now, running his hands through his thinning grey hair, 'and tired. I need to start thinking about the future.'

'I quite agree,' Courtney said, glad that he understood why she was so upset at Uncle Leander's scheming. 'That's what I thought. That's why I was so worried when Uncle Leander started...'

'Oh, bother Leander,' her father said brusquely. 'Leander is in league with the devil, always has been, always will be. I want nothing to do with him.'

'No, of course not. But the money from the trust...'

'The money from the trust isn't relevant either,' Endicott said firmly. 'What I need is peace of mind.'

Courtney looked at him carefully. 'Peace of mind?'

'To know that my work is being carried on in the best fashion possible.'

'Well, I'm sure it will be,' she said confidently. 'I mean, I hear Robert is everything you could ask for.'

'Everything,' her father agreed. He fixed her with a benign blue stare. 'There's only one thing that would make it perfect.'

Courtney didn't need to ask what it was. Her fingers clenched into fists. She glared at the ground between her feet.

'I do so hate to see all the Lord's work go to waste because Robert doesn't have the respect of the people the way I have.'

'I think everyone respects him a lot,' Courtney countered.

'But not the way they would if he were married. Married to the right woman.'

She didn't say a word. That was one line he couldn't expect her to feed him, could he?

'You.'

Subtle he was not. Courtney knew she shouldn't even be surprised. It was only to be expected. Had she really thought her father would have changed, would have considered her happiness, her needs, her desires, for once in his life? Well, if she had, however fleetingly, she was wrong.

'I'm marrying Aidan, Daddy.'

He reached down and lifted her chin with his hands, staring down into her eyes. She swallowed hard, praying that God believed more in free will than her father did, and also that He would forgive her the lie.

'I'm asking you once and for all, do you love him?' Endicott Perkins demanded in his pulpit voice. And there was no way she could lie to that tone.

'Yes,' she confessed. 'I do.'

And, God help her, she did. She loved the insufferable jerk despite his authoritative, overbearing, rude, obnoxious behaviour. She loved him despite his mocking eyes, his sarcastic comments, his sardonic smile.

'And you couldn't love Robert instead?' her father asked in a last-ditch hope.

'No. I could not.'

He sighed, hauled himself wearily to his feet. He stood above her and regarded her almost sadly. 'I tried,' he said to the treetops where presumably the Almighty was hiding. 'I'll tell your mother then,' he said to Courtney as he started back towards the village. 'I do hope you know what you're doing.'

He wasn't the only one, Courtney thought as she watched him walk away.

The one thing Courtney had always admired about her parents was their flexibility. They never knew what was coming next in their lives. Frequently it wasn't what they had planned—not even her father, who planned better than anyone she knew. But whatever happened, they adjusted.

And within twenty-four hours after her father's last attempt to bring her around, her parents had adjusted to her marrying Aidan.

Her mother stopped her outside the hut the next morning and gave her a warm, maternal hug. 'I just want you to know I've made my peace with it,' she said. 'I understand.'

Momentarily baffled, Courtney frowned. 'Peace with what?'

'Your marriage. Your loving Aidan. I've thought about it a lot, and it is like my love for Chippy. You're a one-man woman, just like me.'

Courtney relayed the acceptance, though not its form, to Aidan when they went out on a foraging expedition with Robert and several of the native men.

'Now, if only Daddy would,' she said.

Aidan grunted, bending his head to avoid a low-hanging branch as they walked along. He seemed to have regained his slightly mocking outlook on life now, and whatever had been tormenting him the day before didn't seem to be bothering him at the moment. He was basically polite and essentially uncommunicative. And it suited Courtney fine.

Now that she had realised she loved him, she didn't want any more *tête-à-tête* encounters with him than were necessary. What she needed was to come up with an excuse for them to leave as soon as possible, so that she could leave Aidan and the Amazon behind, returning to California with her heart intact.

'Maybe Daddy will give you his blessing this evening,' Aidan said.

'I hope so,' Courtney prayed.

He was, in fact, waiting for them when they got back. 'Have a good morning?' he asked them, smiling.

'Very.' Courtney put a net full of grapes on the make-shift table. 'And I don't think you need to worry about Robert coping with the tribe,' she added. 'I think he gets along just fine.'

'I suppose you may be right,' Endicott agreed.

'And when the right wife comes along, I'm sure he'll know,' Courtney tacked on, just to cement her position.

Her father nodded sagely. 'I'm sure you're right about that, too.' He closed his Bible and smiled at them beneficently. 'The Lord will provide.'

'Yes,' Courtney agreed happily. It seemed as if her prayers had been answered.

'In the meantime, I've found that He has provided something else.'

'Oh, yes?'

'Yes, indeed. A true demonstration of the joy of holy matrimony.' He rubbed his hands together in gleeful anticipation.

'Huh?'

'The entire tribe will simply witness *your* wedding instead.'

CHAPTER EIGHT

Wedding?

'D...did you say *wedding*, Daddy?'

Endicott beamed. 'Yes, of course I did. Don't know why I didn't think of it before. Doesn't matter *who* you marry. Just need you to marry someone.'

'...Doesn't...matter?' Courtney echoed faintly. Her voice wasn't the only thing about to faint. Her knees felt as if they were about to melt beneath her.

'Not a bit,' her father assured her cheerfully, giving her a conspiratorial squeeze. 'Of course, it would be best if you were going to marry Robert, but...' He sighed as if, were he arranging the world, he would have done a better job of it. 'It's more than Robert we're concerned about here. It's the affirmation of holy matrimony that's important. An example of marital commitment. I must be able to have a concrete example to point to. So——' he gave her a wide smile '—a wedding there will be.'

Courtney stared at him, still dumbfounded, unable even to come up with one word that would contradict everything he had just said and not make life worse in the process.

Her father's brows drew together as he seemed to notice from the expression on her face that something was amiss. 'Oh, you don't have to worry about it. Your mother and I will make all the plans.'

'Daddy, I——' she tried.

But Endicott made shooing motions with his hands. 'Go on now, both of you. And smile, for goodness' sake. It's what you've been wanting, isn't it?'

Was it?

Good lord, the idea of actually marrying Aidan Sawyer boggled the mind. Courtney licked her suddenly parched lips and looked at her sham fiancé. Where were Aidan and his 'save-the-day' lines now? she wondered irritably. He looked, if possible, more stunned than she did. He had gone quite white around the mouth, and Courtney could see a muscle jumping in his tightly clenched jaw. A thin film of perspiration beaded his forehead.

'Of course, Daddy,' she said hollowly and, grabbing Aidan's hand, she hauled him out of the hut before he could pass out on the spot.

'Way to go,' she hissed at him the moment they were alone in the round.

He blinked, then stared at her, uncomprehending. 'What do you mean by that?'

'I mean this is all your fault!'

'Mine?' His outrage was obvious. *'Mine?'*

'Yours,' she insisted. 'You said you were my fiancé!'

'You said you were getting married!'

She glared at him. 'I didn't say to whom.'

'No, your daddy was going to do that for you. And if I hadn't said it was me, it would have been dear old Robert, and you know it.'

The trouble was, she did know it, much as she would rather not. Slapping her hands on her hips, she scowled at him. 'That's neither here nor there,' she said gruffly. 'The question is, what are we going to do now?'

'Are you two arguing, darlings?' Marguerite appeared suddenly just behind them, putting her arms around them both. 'You mustn't, you know.'

'Mustn't what?' Aidan growled.

'Argue.' She shook her head, tisk-tisking reprovingly. 'Sets a very bad example. And you haven't a thing to worry about. Chippy and I will take care of everything. I do love weddings. And I'll especially love yours. My own daughter, married at last. I'm so glad you came to tell us in person. I wouldn't miss it for the world.' She gave them both a squeeze and vanished into the hut saying, 'Chippy, I have just the hymns picked out.'

'Oh, lord,' Courtney muttered, but before she could follow her mother and put an end to the nonsense, Aidan grabbed her hand and dragged her away. She let him drag her, even though she imagined he was going to haul her off into the jungle and throttle her. She wouldn't have blamed him. He certainly hadn't bargained on this.

Neither of them had bargained on this.

'He means it, doesn't he?' Aidan asked after he had cast about for a suitable refuge and had finally settled on his sleeping hut.

'Yes,' she agreed. 'He means it.' She looked around the hut nervously, not having been in it before.

Aidan made an explosive sound and began pacing, his jaw working, his breathing rough. He didn't speak, just fumed silently. Finally he slammed his fist against one of the uprights and said a very rude word. Then he bent down and riffled through his duffel bag and rooted out the bottle of *cachaça*. He sloshed two healthy doses into the tin cups on the table. 'Here.' He thrust one of the cups into her hand. 'Drink this.'

Courtney looked at it, then at him. His expression had gone from stunned to furious.

Surprise, she thought glumly. And guess who he was mad at. 'I'm sorry,' she mumbled, then took refuge behind the cup, swallowing rapidly, then coughing as the *cachaça* did its work on her.

Aidan jerked the cup out of her hand and slapped her on the back, making her cough harder.

'I'm all right!' she choked, trying to shove him away. But he held her too tightly, his fingers almost bruising her upper arms, his eyes bright with anger as he glared down into hers. 'I'm all right,' she repeated slowly, which was a lie. She could never be this close to him and be all right. 'It was just a shock.'

Aidan's hands dropped and he regarded her curiously. 'It's a shock all right,' he muttered and she knew he didn't mean the liquor.

'Daddy means well,' she began, trying to defend her father yet again.

'Does he?' Aidan was obviously sceptical.

'He's concerned about the mission.'

He gave her a long, assessing stare, as if he were trying to decide if she should be committed or not. Finally he shook his head. 'You don't care?'

'About the mission? Of course, I——'

'Not about the mission! About you!'

'Me?'

'That he sees your wedding as just some religious three-ring circus!'

Courtney shrugged. There was no way to explain her father. 'It's just the way he is.'

Aidan snorted and slugged back the rest of the cup of *cachaça*. 'Whatever you say,' he said finally. He stretched out on the hammock and shut his eyes.

Courtney pursed her lips as she twisted the cup round and round in her hands. She wished she had the courage simply to tell her father it was all a mistake.

She had to. She couldn't simply marry a man for convenience sake, could she? Of course not.

Or could she? People used to do it all the time, she told herself. To consolidate properties or to unite families. And then they fell madly in love with each other, and then on page 186 the author got to write 'The End', and no one had to worry if it worked out or not.

But in real life? Hardly.

And especially not with Aidan Sawyer. A man who had already been trapped into one marriage surely wouldn't relish another. She wouldn't have to do anything, she decided glumly. Aidan would do it for her. There was no way he was going to let himself get trapped a second time. No way on earth.

So how are we going to get out of this one? she wanted to ask him, but just then she heard a trilling, 'Yoo hoo, Courtney,' from beyond the wall of the hut, and seconds later her mother poked her head around the corner of the door. 'Oh good, you are here. Your father and I have sorted out the hymns. Now I want to talk to you about your dress.'

Courtney groaned. 'Mother, I——'

'Now don't tell me that just because we're in the middle of the jungle that this shouldn't be a wedding to be proud of. We're going to do it right, you know. We must. It will be an occasion to remember. Come along. Jacinta is quite a talented seamstress,' she said, referring to one of the Indian women to whom she had been teaching a variety of Western skills. 'I think she might have some ideas for us.'

And before Courtney could do more than give Aidan a backward glance, she was borne off by her mother to discuss wedding plans.

All day long she expected he would approach her father and tell him the whole thing was a mistake. All day long she sat outside her parents' hut with Jacinta and her mother and let the half-Portuguese, half-Indian discussion wash over her, ignoring all the plans for her own wedding, waiting for Aidan to come and tell her father and mother that they were all unnecessary: there wasn't going to be any wedding.

Aidan didn't come out of the hut for almost an hour after she and her mother had left him. Probably finishing off the bottle of *cachaça*, she thought grimly. She would have if she had had access to it. She stiffened, fully expecting him to stride over and demand to talk to her father, but he didn't even glance her way. He headed directly across the round and disappeared down the path towards the river. She stared after him, half dismayed, half confused.

He didn't return by dinner time. She would have liked to ask someone where he was, but as his fiancée, she figured that they would wonder at her not knowing. So she picked at her food and answered her mother's continuing questions in monosyllables, wishing all the time that she had never begun this whole farce.

'Where is your young man, then?' her father asked her after they had eaten and Courtney was helping clean up.

Before she could confess her ignorance, one of the Indian men said something, pointing towards the river. Endicott frowned. Courtney wasn't sure what the man had said, but she felt a momentary jolt of apprehension.

'What is it?' she asked her father.

'Pãolo says he's gone. He took the boat.'

The apprehension turned to a full-blooded panic. Aidan had left her? Without even a word or a backward glance? The panic flared into anger, and she lurched to her feet.

She shouldn't have been surprised. She knew Aidan Sawyer wouldn't like being trapped. But he could have said! He could have just told her to call it off. He didn't have to run out on her!

Unthinking, she began to run, ignoring the shouted question from her father and the curious stares of the people she passed. She had to get to the river, had to see for herself that he had really left.

It had just gone dusk and the jungle path was shadowed and overhung, making it impossible to see more than a foot or two ahead. It was the time for jaguars to begin roaming, for tapirs to go down to the riverbanks. But she didn't care. She had no thought beyond the fear that Aidan had left her. Keeping her head down, she ploughed on, heedless of the scrambling monkeys overhead and the tree frogs who stopped their shrill noise as she passed. She had to know. Had to check. Had to——

'Oof!'

Strong, hard arms came around her. 'Hey!'

'You!' Oh God, it was. Hot, pulsing relief surged through her, dizzying her. Breathing in the musky, male smell of him, she wilted against the solid warmth of Aidan's chest.

'Hey, hey.' The words were softer now, comforting almost, as if he could feel the swift throb of her heart in her chest, as if her trembling had communicated her unspoken fears. 'What's wrong?' Aidan drew her tightly in his arms for a moment, then held her away from him to gaze sternly down into her face. 'What did he do now?'

'He? Do? Who?'

He shook his head, apparently as baffled by her reactions as she was by his. 'Never mind. What's wrong? What's up?'

'I—I thought——' She couldn't tell him she thought he had left her. Couldn't betray her fears. He would hate it, feel obliged by it, trapped. 'I—just needed to get away.'

He gave a wry half-laugh. 'Yeah, well, if you've been planning the wedding of the century all afternoon, I can understand that.'

She gave him a weak smile, grateful that he had hit upon his own explanation for her outrageous behaviour. But she was still shivering inside and she didn't try to step away just yet, afraid that her legs wouldn't hold her.

'You all right now?'

She nodded, still unable to speak. Her heart was hammering in her chest.

'You ready to go back? Or do you want to sit awhile?'

'No, I can go back.' As long as you're here, she added silently. She squared her shoulders and fell into step beside him. 'Where'd you go?' she ventured finally. 'One of the men said you'd . . . you'd left . . . in the boat.' She couldn't begin to tell him the terror she had felt. It was crazy, insane, all out of proportion to what she knew their relationship was destined to be. He was just the man who was helping her out of a tight situation, wasn't he? And not a very willing one at that. But she couldn't stop the shivers that ran through her, and she found herself snuggling more closely beneath the arm that had looped itself over her shoulders.

That arm over her shoulders tightened just then and gave her a squeeze. 'I went out for a cruise.'

'You could have taken me with you,' she said gruffly.

He gave her a wry look. 'No, I couldn't.'

'Why not?'

But he didn't answer because just then Robert and two of the Indian men came towards them and Robert said, 'Oh, you found him, then,' and Courtney nodded.

Aidan's brow lifted. 'You were looking?'

She ducked her head, embarrassed to answer, not wanting to give him the idea that she was trapping him any more than she already was.

'Were you?' he persisted.

She frowned and said irritably, 'Well, you'd been gone for hours. Everyone wondered where you were.'

'Of course.' But the look he gave her was speculative all the same.

Over the next three days Courtney gained a new appreciation of the theological concept of limbo. She felt as if she were in a state of suspended animation—dragged into discussions of wedding plans for a wedding she was certain would never take place.

The wedding that was never going to take place, she discovered the following morning, was scheduled for Saturday.

'But it's Wednesday now!' she protested in vain to her mother.

Marguerite was singularly unsympathetic. 'Well, you're the one who said you had to hurry back and get this letter to Leander.'

'I do,' Courtney maintained. She had tried once or twice to use her need to get back to Leander with some proof of her father's earthly existence as a reason to persuade her parents that there really wasn't time for a jungle wedding. She and Aidan could easily get married when they were back in the States, she argued.

Her parents wouldn't hear of it. She was their only daughter and they were going to do it right. Not to mention, of course, how well it fitted into her father's spiritual plans. And wasn't it luck, Marguerite had remarked, that they could do all the preparations themselves and would not have to worry about caterers and flowers and bridesmaids and receptions. Things could come about so much more quickly this way.

That was, in fact, how they had decided upon Saturday.

'Then you'll still be able to spend a few days with us before you have to get back to the States,' her mother said. 'It will be lovely. Honestly, darling, you worry too much.'

Courtney supposed there was some truth to that. She was worrying every minute of every day. She worried what she would do if Aidan told her father it was all a lie, and then she worried what she would do if he didn't.

She expected every moment of every day that he would come and tell her that it was all off. And she was amazed every moment that went by and he didn't.

She began to wonder why.

She wanted to ask him, but she wasn't sure she wanted to hear his answer.

Unless.

Unless he was coming to love her the way she had learned to love him.

Fat chance.

But still, what other reason would he have for persisting in the charade, unless he wanted it to be real? She leaned back against the outside wall of one of the huts and scowled as she thought about it.

It wasn't the sort of thing she liked letting herself do, wallowing in make-believe this way. Not unless she could get a book out of it anyway. And she couldn't get a book out of this, that was certain. Still she couldn't stop tipping her head back and closing her eyes, letting the soft sounds of the children playing and the women chatting while they worked play over her while she thought about the possibility of marrying an Aidan Sawyer who loved her.

It was altogether too tempting—and too likely to lead absolutely nowhere. But the feelings she got around Aidan Sawyer were a far cry from anything she had felt about Clarke or any of his predecessors, and she couldn't help the way he made her feel. All the other men she had known had all been too stodgy, bland and set in their ways for her. They had looked at her stubborn chin and had shaken their heads. Or they had taken her spirit and tried to break it or mould it to suit theirs.

Only Aidan had fought her nose to nose. He might have resented her coercing him into bringing her, but he had done it. And when things had got rough, he had come to her rescue. As she had come to his. They were suited, she told herself.

But there wasn't any future in it.

Unless he had undergone a miraculous transformation—a transformation that seemed highly unlikely considering the fact that he hadn't even smiled at her in days—chances were not good.

She glanced across the compound at him now. He was laughing and talking with three Indian men. He had been sitting there for the last hour, and he hadn't so much as looked at her. She looked at him gloomily. Then her gaze drifted to two little children chasing a rooster in the dirt.

In the past, childish occupations like that had only reminded her of her own past, giving her memories that were frequently the starting point of some story or other. Now they made her think of the future—of the possibility of children of her own.

Aidan's children?

'Stop it,' she muttered aloud and, hauling herself to her feet, she went inside the hut to see if she couldn't coerce her mother into finding something for her to do.

But all the time she was washing the clothes her mother had found for her, she kept right on thinking about the impossible. And hoping.

Perhaps he would come to her and tell her he meant it to be more than a sham. Perhaps he would tell her that he had fallen in love with her after all. And perhaps her father would wake up some morning and decide he wasn't cut out to save the world.

Not likely, any of them.

*   *   *

The day of the wedding dawned under the threat of a torrential rainstorm. Suitable, Courtney thought, as she stared out of the door of the hut. Maybe they could call it off, like a baseball game. How many weddings had been called off because of rain?

None. And this wasn't going to be the first, and she knew it. Nothing would stop her father from performing the ceremony precisely at ten o'clock, not even another of Noah's floods. It would go on as scheduled ... unless Aidan left her at the altar.

The possibility occurred to her almost hourly. Though whether she was worried that he would or that he wouldn't, she didn't know for sure. She could imagine the whole situation in vivid detail, right up to when she would walk out of the hut and across the compound to where her father would be standing, waiting for her. And when she would look for Aidan, no one would be there.

He had given no sign that he intended to abandon her. But what did that signify? Though her experience with such things was not great, she doubted if many men who bolted at the last minute dropped blatant hints beforehand. And he certainly couldn't be marrying her unwillingly. Could he? For the thousandth time she wished she knew the answer to that question.

Her hand shook as she brushed her hair and the brush fell to the ground. Only two hours until the fateful moment. Jacinta, who had been like her shadow ever since her mother had started planning the wedding, pounced on it and handed it back to her.

'You worry?' she asked Courtney, a smile lighting her dark face.

'Yes.' At least she didn't have to lie about that. It was all right for brides to be panicky, though not for her reasons.

'Come eat something,' Jacinta urged her. 'You feel better.'

'Yes, do,' Marguerite encouraged, taking in her daughter's pale face and trembling hands.

Courtney shook her head. 'I couldn't. I—don't feel too well.'

Marguerite smiled benignly. 'It's only nerves. I felt the same way the day I was marrying Chippy.'

Courtney doubted that her parents' wedding had been even remotely like this one, but she didn't say so. She just went on numbly brushing her hair until it shone golden in the stormy shadows of the mid-morning light.

'A little food in your stomach will do you good,' Marguerite insisted, thrusting a bowl of spicy vegetable soup into her hands.

Soup she couldn't face. But seeing that she wasn't going to escape without something, she reached for some grapes and popped one into her mouth. 'I think I'll take some to Aidan,' she said quickly, needing an excuse to escape.

'It's bad luck, sweetie,' her mother cautioned.

What could be worse? Courtney wondered. But she merely shook her head and said, 'I'll tell him to hide his eyes.'

Once she had got away from her mother and the ever-present Jacinta, she thought that seeing Aidan was an excellent idea.

She could not, absolutely *could not*, face being left at the altar and having to make explanations there. If he was going to back out at the last minute, he owed it to her to tell her now.

And if he wasn't?

If he wasn't, she wanted to know that, too. And *why*. Crossing her fingers, she strode across the compound and entered his hut.

He was still asleep. She stared, outraged at the in-justice of it. She hadn't slept more than ten minutes all night. Probably not more than ten hours over the past three days. And he was lying there in his hammock, curled on his side, a thin cotton blanket half-way down his chest, which rose and fell with the even breathing of a man who didn't have a care in the world.

She walked around the hammock, staring at him from both sides, trying to decide how she should wake him...*if* she should wake him. Once she walked to the door, then came back and stood glowering down on his sleeping form. With her luck he wouldn't leave before the wedding, he would just sleep right through it!

And what would her father—and his parishioners—think then?

She reached out and took hold of his foot and shook him firmly. He scowled fiercely and twitched away from her, grumbling in his sleep. She tugged again.

'Ahem!'

He blinked, then opened his eyes and frowned at her from beneath the mosquito netting. 'Oh, it's you. What d'you want?' His voice was gruff with sleep.

'I brought you some grapes.' She held them out.

He shook his head, baffled. 'You woke me up for that?'

'I need to talk to you.'

He rubbed his hands through his already spiky hair, then squinted at her. 'Why?'

'Why?'

'Why?' he repeated, as if it were a perfectly sane question. He rubbed a hand over his face, scratching absently at the stubbly beard that had been growing for the past few days.

'You do know what today is, don't you?'

'Saturday?' he ventured.

'Yes. It's Saturday,' she agreed through clenched teeth, feeling as if she were talking to a half-wit. 'And what happens on Saturday, do you remember that?'

He straightened out in the hammock and stared up at her implacably. 'We're getting married.' There was absolutely no emotion in his voice.

Courtney felt a tidal wave of emotion swamp her. 'Are we?' She couldn't help it. The question sprang out unbidden.

He went completely still. 'Unless you called it off. Did you?'

'N...no. I...thought...you would.'

He stared at her, his face still not giving anything away. 'No,' he said evenly, 'I didn't.'

'Oh.' She hoped there wasn't as much relief in her voice as she felt in her bones. She gave him what she hoped was a bright smile. 'Well, uh...all right.'

They looked at each other in silence.

Courtney twisted the tails of her shirt nervously. 'I...er, I...that's all I wanted to know, really,' she babbled. 'I just...' she gave a half-hysterical laugh, 'didn't want to be...left at the...altar.'

He looked at her, his eyes blank. 'No.'

She managed a smile again, twisted her shirt tails again, then began backing out of the hut quickly, and knocked over the rickety bookcase that her father had built and which impeded backward progress towards the door.

'Heavens,' she muttered and turned to right it, stuffing the books in haphazardly, feeling her cheeks and the back of her neck burn. She got all the books back in, then flashed a worried glance at Aidan. He hadn't moved.

'Well, I'll...see you later,' she said brightly, giving him a jaunty wave of her hand.

'Yes.'

She was out of the door in a flash, and back a split second later. 'Aidan?'

He looked startled. 'What?'

'Why?'

'Why what?'

'Why are you going through with it?'

He glared at her. 'You need me to.'

'But you don't *have* to,' she argued.

'Would you rather I didn't?'

'No. I mean, yes. I mean...well, you don't have to. I can think of something else,' she went on frantically.

'What?' His voice held an emotion at last—scorn.

She didn't know. She hung her head. Her heart pounded painfully against her ribs. Why hadn't she just left things well alone? Why hadn't she quit while she was ahead? 'I . . . I could think of something,' she said finally.

Aidan snorted.

'You told me you didn't want to be married again,' she went on steadfastly, wishing she would shut up with every word she spoke. 'You said marriage was a trap. So why are you doing it?' *Say you love me,* she pleaded silently. *Tell me that's the reason.*

'It doesn't have to be a trap,' Aidan said calmly and reasonably. 'We can always get it annulled.'

CHAPTER NINE

'DEARLY beloved...'

It was actually happening.

'We are gathered here today...'

She hadn't believed it would, not even at the last instant.

'...to join together this man and this woman in holy matrimony.'

But it was. She and Aidan were standing side by side, stiff and silent, while her father intoned the introductory words of the marriage ceremony. He paused then and smiled at them both, then turned to the assembled congregation, a group of about forty Indians plus his wife and Robert, all equally stiff and silent except for Marguerite's audible sniffs, and repeated the words in the Indian dialect.

Courtney tried to catch a glimpse of Aidan out of the corner of her eye. But the veil her mother had fashioned out of a sheer length of nylon net that someone had traded for and had used to catch bait with made it difficult. But she had no difficulty remembering the white, strained face she had focused on when she had walked in measured steps across the compound to the soft reedy flutes that had played an improvised processional moments before.

'...those who enter into this relation shall cherish a mutual esteem and love,' her father was saying. 'They bear with each other's infirmities and weaknesses, comfort each other...in honesty and industry provide for each other.'

The words, which ought to have been an inspiration, were a condemnation instead. It was hypocrisy. It was wrong. It was a mockery of all that marriage should be. And yet it wasn't.

She did love Aidan. Given the chance, she would cherish him, would bear with him in sickness and pain, would comfort him. In honesty she could promise to be the best wife she could be.

But Aidan wanted no wife.

'Aidan Sawyer, will you take this woman to be your wife?' Endicott directed his gaze at the man who stood beside her. 'Will you pledge your commitment to her in all love and honour, in all duty and service, in all faith and tenderness, to live with her in the holy bond of marriage?'

Courtney couldn't even lift her eyes to watch his face. She could do no more than stare at the dirt between her feet and hold her breath. She only breathed again when she heard the words, emotionless and wooden, 'I will.'

'And you, my daughter...' She knew from her father's voice that he was smiling at her, but she couldn't smile back. She could do nothing except feel the misery of the moment, knowing that she was marrying the man she loved, promising the things she meant most deeply in her heart, and that they were the last words on earth he wanted to hear.

Her father repeated the question he had asked Aidan to her this time, then waited for her response.

She shivered as if the sun had vanished, though the storm had come and gone and it shone brighter than ever. Then she dredged up the words from the bottom of her heart. 'I will.'

Endicott beamed. He reached for her hand which, despite the heat and humidity, felt cold and clammy, and he put it into Aidan's colder, clammier one. 'Please be seated,' he said.

They sat on a makeshift bench, the tribe clustered around, sitting on mats, every eye on Endicott who bowed his head for a moment, shut his eyes, then, taking a breath, lifted his gaze and looked right at the couple seated before him.

'Marriage,' he said in the soft, slow cadences that Courtney remembered from childhood, 'is a commitment. It is a promise. A burden, and yet a joy. It brings with it happiness and it can bring with it hardship. But above all, it must bring with it love.' He looked at them each in turn. Courtney swallowed hard, then, steeling herself, met his gaze. If Aidan did, she had no way of knowing. His hand tightened convulsively around hers.

'It is not,' her father went on sonorously, 'always what we would have it be. And it is not,' he added with a self-deprecating smile, 'always with whom other people would have us marry. But there is a lesson there, too. We must not always think we know best. We must be open, willing to learn, to embrace the things we do not understand, the things we would not have chosen . . . for there is a wisdom beyond ours.'

He folded his hands and smiled down at the couple sitting so stiffly before him. 'It is that wisdom that we celebrate today. It is that commitment we celebrate today. We do not know what the future brings to this marriage, to these two young people. But we pray that they are blessed with happiness, fidelity, the joys of parenthood, long life. We hope earnestly that they will bring these things to each other, enriching each other's lives, cherishing each other as long as they both shall live.'

Courtney felt more vile, more rotten, more perfectly awful than she had ever felt in her life. Because she wanted all those things desperately—wanted them with Aidan—and the whole thing, all her promises, all his, all her father's well chosen words, were a lie. She bowed her head and wished the earth would swallow her up.

'Come now,' her father was saying, beckoning to them. Trembling she got to her feet and Aidan lurched to his. She heard him let out a pent-up breath. She heard him swallow. She felt the slight tremor in his hand which still held hers.

'The vows,' Endicott said, turning to Aidan.

The vows. Compounding the disaster, they promised each other fidelity, love, kindness—everything good and beautiful.

Then Aidan took a ring and slipped it on her finger, repeating the words her father said, 'With this ring, I thee wed.' And their eyes met for the first time since she had walked across the compound. She thought he looked as if he had died.

His expression was hunted, as if he were caught in a trap from which there was no escape, and the only way out was to retreat within himself.

She was glad she had no ring for him. It would only have made things worse.

'I now pronounce you man and wife.' Endicott turned to Aidan. 'You may kiss the bride.'

Marguerite stepped forward and lifted the former fishnet from her daughter's face, turning her bodily so she faced the man who was her husband. He didn't move, just looked at her, stricken.

'Well, go on, man, don't be bashful.' Endicott was chortling now. He gave Aidan a push on the shoulder. 'Kiss your wife.'

Courtney remembered their last kiss—their first kiss. She remembered the warmth, the way the blood sang in her veins, the way her heart hammered and her body had responded to his. She remembered the need she felt, the overpowering ache that had only grown worse when at last he had put her away from him. The colour flared in her cheeks.

Aidan leaned forward, grasped her arms, and bent his head. He licked his lips, then touched them briefly to hers. His hands trembled violently against her. Abruptly he turned away. He looked angry. In pain.

She shouldn't be surprised. There was no love in this for him. No joy. It was a responsibility, one he had felt obliged, probably because of the incident with the jaguar, to take on. And one which, without a doubt, brought him far more painful memories than hers. He was probably thinking of Shanna now, of the vows he had taken and meant, and the farce they turned out to be.

And these vows? These could only be worse for they were a farce to begin with, weren't they?

But she had no time to think further, for her mother was hugging her, her father was beaming, slapping Aidan on the back, telling everyone that they made a wonderful couple, that the wedding was all it should be.

'Don't you think so, my dear?' He turned to Courtney.

'Yes,' she said, not looking at her husband.

What else, after all, could she say?

She went through the afternoon the same way, outwardly smiling, accepting the heartfelt congratulations of Jacinta and her family, the shyly envious looks of one or two of the younger, unmarried women, the genuine approval of the men. And she watched Aidan do the same.

No one would have known that it was painful for him. No one would have guessed that the minute they left here, he would be asking her for an annulment. But he would be, and she knew it. The thought, painful though it was, nagged at the back of her mind.

'We can always get it annulled,' she remembered him saying again, and again the words cut her to the bone. Yet they were only what she should have expected, she told herself. He had never pretended love, only lust. And neither of them would want a marriage based on that. Still, it had hurt to have one's worst fears confirmed. And it hurt again now when her mother paused beside her, in the process of serving the community celebration meal, and said, 'Such a wonderful wedding. What more could anyone ask?'

A groom who loved her, perhaps? But Courtney knew that wasn't a possibility now. It was enough that her father had his wedding, which he had done a wonderful job on, she had to admit. And it was enough that she had avoided making him happy and herself and Robert miserable by agreeing to the marriage he had planned for them. *Smile,* she told herself firmly. So she did just that. But the reception seemed to last for hours.

When it finally wound down at dusk, she began helping Jacinta clear things away, relieved that it was over, tired of being a spectacle and thinking only of the refuge the night would bring.

'Here, here,' her mother said, taking the bowl out of her hands. 'You don't need to do this.'

'I don't mind,' Courtney said and meant it.

But her mother wouldn't believe that. She shook her head, half laughing. 'Perhaps not, but I'm sure Aidan does.'

'What's he got to do with it?'

'He's your husband, and he's waiting for you. To go to bed,' her mother added in a stentorian whisper that nailed Courtney where she stood.

'Mother!'

Her mother patted her cheek. 'Don't be a prude, dear. How do you think I managed to have you?'

Courtney hadn't given it much thought, although given her father's paramount devotion to the duties of his vocation, an immaculate conception didn't seem totally beyond the realm of possibility. 'I—well, I——'

Her mother handed Jacinta the bowl and put her hands on Courtney's shoulders, spinning her daughter around so that she was facing Aidan, who was standing with a group of men who were all laughing and talking across the compound. When he saw her looking at him, the grin faded from his face. His eyes met hers.

'If he was looking at me like that, I wouldn't be wasting time doing the dishes, love,' her mother said, giving her a shove. 'Go on.'

Unable to think of a way out of obeying, Courtney went. The men Aidan was standing with all turned to watch her approach. One of them grinned and said something. The rest laughed and the tallest one punched Aidan lightly in the shoulder. He coloured, then frowned.

'She come to take you away now,' one of them said in Portuguese. 'You go, Aidan. Have a gooooood time.' And they all cackled together.

Aidan scowled fiercely, then reached out and grabbed her hand, hauling her with him into the hut he had been using, out of sight of the men, but not out of sound. One of them continued to speak on the subject, Courtney was certain, for they all laughed and made sounds of passion that turned her a darker red than the man who was now her husband.

What had she been thinking about when she had considered the night to come as a refuge? A false wedding night would be even worse than a false wedding day.

Aidan seemed to think so too. He kicked out a stool for her to sit on and motioned her on to it. Then he got out his rapidly vanishing bottle of *cachaça* and poured them each a glass. He handed one to her, then regarded her solemnly over the rim.

He lifted the glass in an ironic toast, but said nothing. What was there to say? To us, perhaps? Hardly. To annulments? Perhaps.

'To getting through the night,' he said harshly and, tipping his head back, drained the cup in one long swallow.

Courtney nodded. She could drink to that. She took a healthy swallow herself and felt the heat all the way to her toes.

Aidan poured himself another cup and held out the bottle to her. She shook her head. He shrugged and sank down on the hammock, cradling his cup in his hands, contemplating the dark liquid. At last he lifted his eyes to meet hers. The vivid jade colour always astonished her, so intense were they in the dark tan of his face, and even more so now in the dim light of the hut. He pressed his lips together for a moment, then expelled a long breath.

'Your mother moved your stuff over here.'

Nonplussed, Courtney stared at him, then followed his gaze to the far side of the hut where she saw her duffel bag leaning against a low table. 'What about my hammock?'

His mouth twisted. 'She didn't bring that.'

'I'll go and get it.'

'Sure, and then what will they think?'

'Well, where else am I...' But she didn't even need to finish the question. It was all too clear where everyone expected her to sleep, where any bride would sleep—with her husband.

She gulped the last of her *cachaça*, then took the bottle from the floor where he had set it and poured herself some more. But even the second cupful didn't do a lot towards restoring her equanimity.

Sleep with Aidan Sawyer?

That was what she had been avoiding for days.

'You said you wanted an annulment.' She glared at him accusingly.

He glared back. 'I do.'

'Well, you won't get one if we...we...' She gave a vague wave of her hand. It was the *cachaça* that was making her burn, she told herself, not the idea of sharing a hammock with Aidan Sawyer.

'We won't,' he growled. He lurched to his feet and began pacing around the inside of the small hut like a caged animal. 'But they can't know that.'

'No,' Courtney agreed promptly.

'We'll just have to make it look good.'

'Yes.'

He scowled at her. 'Pity you weren't so accommodating a week ago, we wouldn't be in this mess.'

'I didn't make you marry me!'

He snorted, not even bothering to answer that. He strode across the room and rooted through his own duffel bag. 'I'm going down to the river for a wash and a swim. You'd better come along, too.'

'But, I——'

'Objecting already? I knew it was too good to last. Come on,' he commanded. 'A newly married woman wouldn't miss the chance of a bath with her husband.'

'I'm missing it.'

He yanked her duffel bag up on to the table and searched through it, pulling out a towel and her toilet kit. Tossing them to her, he said, 'Suit yourself. Sit on the bank for all I care. But you're coming with me.'

His was not a temper to argue with. She went with him.

After all, if he wanted to strip naked in front of her, who was she to complain? Remembering her earlier peeping, she ought to be pleased.

He stopped long enough to say something to the men who were now sitting on the ground in a circle, smoking and talking, passing a bottle of *cachaça* among themselves. Whatever he said to them, they beamed and nodded, and when Courtney followed him, head high, down the path to the river, they stared after her and whistled.

'You take your time,' the one who spoke Portuguese shouted after them.

It didn't take a genius to figure out that they thought more than bathing was going to take place.

Nothing more than bathing did, though.

Just bathing—or rather, watching Aidan bathe—was bad enough, Courtney discovered. All her good intentions went for naught. Her ability to keep her eyes averted was nil. Aidan had scarcely stripped off and dived into the water when she found her gaze turning towards him.

It was nearly dark, but his skin, dark in the sunlight, seemed luminous now. His naked back gleamed under the silvery light of the moon, and she found that, once she had begun to look at him, she couldn't look away.

He was primally, essentially male, every inch of him. And the longer she sat there on the log, staring at him, the more conscious she was of it. It was not the best way to preserve the platonic relationship they both desired.

It was odd, she thought, ironic in fact, that Aidan would have gladly gone to bed with her before he had married her. But now that he had become her husband, he vowed not to touch her.

'So, how are we going to manage?' she asked when they got back to the hut and were staring at each other in the dim light of the kerosene lantern that sat on the bookshelf near the door.

Aidan shrugged. He considered her, considered the hammock, then slowly looked around the rest of the small room. The possibilities were not promising. One did not sleep on the ground in the jungle. If one did, there was no guessing what one might find oneself sleeping with by morning. And the tabletop, being barely three feet square, was no more promising.

'I don't see that we have much choice,' he said grimly. His eyes lit on the hammock again.

Courtney sighed. 'Probably not.' She could barely look at him. Memories of what he had looked like naked in the moonlight still haunted her. And it didn't help that he said,

'I don't sleep in anything.'

'You did in the jungle,' she protested.

'Outside, yeah. In here, no.'

'You could tonight.'

He gave her a long hard look, then sighed. 'Yeah, and I'd probably better, too,' he said, which had the effect of making her more nervous than ever.

She had been sleeping in a light cotton shift since she had arrived at her parents' village. It wasn't much protection, but when she started towards the hammock still wearing her wedding dress, Aidan said sharply, 'You're not wearing that, for God's sake.' So she had ducked behind a screen and had changed.

He didn't look at her at all when she emerged in the pale blue shift. 'You get in first. I'll turn out the light.'

Apprehensively, she did as she was told. Aidan crossed the room and put out the light, plunging them into almost total blackness. A relief, Courtney decided, until a moment later he was slipping into the hammock next to her.

There was no way not to touch him. Hammocks simply brought people together no matter what. And now this one was bringing the long hard length of Aidan's body fully and warmly against hers. He had kept on the khakis and long-sleeved shirt he wore, but even those along with her thin cotton shift camouflaged nothing. They could as easily have been nude. His body was branding hers, burning hers. He shifted. She moved. He twitched. She writhed.

'Christ, it's hot,' he muttered.

'Boiling,' she said.

She felt his arm moved up against her, rustling around and she snapped, 'What are you doing?'

'Unbuttoning my shirt.'

'Oh.'

They lay then in silence, listening to the tree frogs, to the skitter and screech of monkeys in the jungle beyond. But mostly they listened to one another's breathing.

'I'm suffocating,' Aidan complained. He sat up and stripped off his shirt, then lay back down. The heat of his arm as it slipped around her raised Courtney's temperature a few degrees as well. She wished she were sleeping in her clothes, then was glad she hadn't. She was burning, and whether it was because of sharing the hammock or because of the heat of the night she didn't want to guess.

It was probably just because of Aidan. And she didn't want to think about that either. She squirmed, trying to get comfortable, to get cool. It didn't work.

'For God's sake, quit that,' Aidan growled.

'Quit what?'

'Wriggling.'

'I'm not!'

'No?'

'No.'

He snorted in clear disagreement. She snorted to repudiate his snort. Then once more they lay in silence, their bodies touching from ear to knee, his arm under her head, his hip hard against hers.

Married to each other. Wanting each other. Even Courtney could admit that to herself now. But neither daring to make a move. For more than wanting her, Aidan wanted an annulment. And no matter what Courtney wanted, she owed him that.

The soft shuffling of feet passed their hut. She heard the low-pitched voice of one of the men saying something and the responding laugh of his wife. She felt Aidan's arm tighten under her head. His body tensed. She turned her head slightly so that she could just make out his profile in the darkness.

'What'd they say?' she asked him.

'Nothing.' His tone was harsh.

'It wasn't nothing,' she contradicted softly.

He muttered an expletive under his breath.

'I suppose I can guess,' she said.

'I suppose you can.'

She smiled a little wryly. 'Well, you must admit, what they expect is closer to what the average wedding night is all about than this is.'

'What do you know about the average wedding night?' He sounded bitter, and she remembered that he had already had one. The thought was oddly painful. Knowing what she did about his previous marriage, it shouldn't have been. But the notion of him having been in love with Shanna then, of having spent the night making love to her, hurt more than she liked to admit.

'I don't know much, I guess.' She tried to make her voice light, but some of the awkwardness she felt obviously crept through.

He sighed heavily. 'I'm sorry. I suppose it isn't your ideal wedding night either, is it?'

It would be, she thought, if he loved her. But she shook her head slightly. 'No.'

He sighed and went silent. For a time neither of them spoke. Then he turned his head slightly so that his lips almost brushed against her hair. 'Did you have an ideal wedding in your mind?'

She stared up at the dark thatch above her head. 'An ideal wedding?' she said a bit dreamily, letting her mind drift on the notion. 'Yeah, I guess I must have.'

'And today wasn't it.'

It wasn't a question, but she felt obliged to defend what had happened today, sham though it might have been. 'It might not have been my fairy-tale wedding, but it was beautiful in its own way.'

Aidan didn't agree or disagree with that. Probably because he didn't want to hurt her feelings, she thought. Then eventually he said in a quiet voice, 'Yes, it was.'

He rolled on to his side so that he was facing her. Her breast touched his arm. She tried to edge back but it wasn't possible, the curve of the hammock's net pressed them together.

'Tell me how you would have planned it,' he said. 'What would you have liked.'

'Besides a husband who loved me, you mean?' She tried to make it sound facetious.

He went suddenly still. 'Besides that.'

'Well, I think I'd have liked a little country wedding. You know the sort. In a white clapboard church with a tall, narrow steeple, hills all around. Lots of grass and flowers. All my dearest friends from my whole life there to share the happiness with me.' She paused. 'Not too likely, I'm afraid. My dearest friends are a motley bunch and they're spread all over the world.'

'We're just imagining,' he said easily. 'What else?'

'A simple dress. White with *broderie anglaise*. Bouquets of daisies. I've always loved daisies.' She rose up slightly on one elbow to look at him as best she could. 'When you got married, did you have daisies?'

'Daisies?' He sounded incredulous. His voice was rough, too, as if it hurt to remember. 'Hardly. We had roses. Red roses. Tons of 'em. And there was nothing simple about any of it. Pomp and circumstance. Silk and taffeta. It wasn't the dress, but how much money it cost that mattered to Shanna.' He flung himself over on to his back again, shaking the hammock so that they swung erratically.

'I'm sorry,' Courtney said quickly. 'I shouldn't have brought it up.'

She felt him shrug. 'It doesn't mater. It's over. Forget it.' He shifted again so that his back was to her this time. 'Go to sleep.'

And that, she thought grimly, was that.

'I'll try.'

She tried. They both tried. But dawn came before sleep did. And when the first faint rays of morning light crept through the rough walls of the hut she shifted on to her back and found herself staring into Aidan's bloodshot eyes and stubbled face. The nearness of him overwhelmed her, and she pulled back.

'Did you sleep?' she asked him.

'Are you kidding?'

The intimacy of their position irritating her now that it was light enough to see, she snapped, 'Well, it's not my fault.'

'Of course not,' he answered just as fractiously.

'It's not!'

'Right.'

She swung her legs over the edge of the hammock and moved to get out. 'I'll just get up then,' she said, 'and let you get your beauty rest.' She slapped her hands on her hips and glared at him. 'Enjoy it, Mr Sawyer.'

'You might as well call me Aidan now that we're married.' He grinned at her annoyance, his vanishing in a flash. Then he reached out a hand and yanked her back in. She fell across his chest, then scrabbled to pull away, but he held her fast.

'Take it easy,' he admonished as she clawed at him, the heat of his body doing terrible things to the desire she had been fighting down all night.

'What are you doing?'

'Keeping you here.'

'Why? I thought you wanted sleep?'

'It would be lovely,' he said, 'but I want us to look like newlyweds more. And you should too, unless you want one of Daddy's sermons on marital bliss,' he told her flatly. 'So we're going to look like we're exhausted from a night of passion, and not be up and running out of the hut at the first crack of sunshine.' He pressed her head against his chest, and she could hear the steady thump of his heart. 'Lie down and relax. We're falling asleep in each other's arms whether we want to or not and we're not coming out of this hut till midday. If then.'

'You're joking.' She lifted her head and stared at him.

'No.' He pressed a palm against her back, moulding her body more fully against his. 'I'm damned well not.'

The strength of his hold and the firmness of his tone told her that he meant every word of it. She sighed. The solid warmth of his body tempted her. And the sleepless night was getting to her. She couldn't fight it—couldn't fight *him*. Didn't even want to try.

'You going to do it?' he asked, his voice soft in her ear.

'I guess.' She tried to sound off-hand. She was enchanted with the view from his shoulder down across the muscled chest and belly to where the waistband of his trousers rode low on his hips.

'That's better. This is at least going to be a morning after for the books.' He paused and sighed.

Courtney raised her head and looked down into his face. 'What's the matter?'

'Books.'

'What about them?'

His mouth twisted wryly. 'I was just thinking about books—about you and your children's books.'

'How so?'

The grin became almost painful. 'They all get married and live happily ever after, don't they? In books?'

She didn't want to think about that.

Happily ever after was precisely what her parents expected from them. And for some reason Aidan seemed determined to see that they got it—even if it killed him and Courtney in the process.

It very nearly did. They almost died of sleeplessness. And desire. And frustration.

The nearness. The wanting. The sharing every night of the hammock that demanded togetherness. Everything conspired against them.

Especially her parents. While before the wedding they had hovered around, talking, smiling, making suggestions, wanting to get to know Aidan better, wanting to catch up on Courtney's news, now they were the souls of discretion.

Now they seemed to vanish for hours at a time. Whenever Courtney came and offered to help wash or sew or teach the children something, her mother shooed her away.

'It's your honeymoon, darling,' she said time and time again. 'You spend it with your husband. I understand.'

She didn't, of course. No one did. Except, strangely enough, Robert.

The third day when Courtney was trying to avoid Aidan in the evening so that they didn't end up together in the hammock any earlier than they had to and so was sitting in the shadows where her mother couldn't see her, weaving a mat out of reeds for one of the Indian women, Robert came up and dropped down beside her.

'How's marriage?' he asked, giving her a smile.

Caught with her guard down by the suddenness of his question, it took her a moment to get her mask of good cheer in place. 'Just fine,' she said brightly.

But he just shook his head as if he doubted her and said, 'Honeymooning *en famille* isn't easy, is it?'

Found out, she agreed. 'Not very, I guess.'

He tipped his head back and leaned against the wall of the hut. 'I wouldn't think so. Glad it's you and him rather than you and me.'

She gave him a sideways look, surprised somewhat.

'You know,' he went on, 'if I were you, I'd get a move on. You don't have to hang around here. You might end up divorced before you leave if you do.'

Her stare was open now. 'What do you mean?'

'I mean all this enforced togetherness with forty people looking over your shoulder. It can't be the best of all possible honeymoons.'

'No.' There was no denying that. And no need to, thank heavens.

'So, go.'

'I'd love to, but...' She gave an ineffectual wave of her hand, trying to make a gesture sum up her frustrations in all her dealings with her parents.

'Don't worry. You made them happy by being married here—even if it wasn't to me. Now make yourself—and Aidan—happy. Get out of here and enjoy your marriage by yourselves.'

'I'd love to,' Courtney said, unsure whether she meant it or not. On the one hand, she would have done it in a minute if her marriage to Aidan had been what everyone thought it was. On the other, she wanted to stay, to prolong the little she had as long as she could.

But that was foolish and she knew it. The sooner they cut their bond, the better for both of them. For Aidan because freedom was what he wanted in the first place; and for her because the sooner she was apart from him, the sooner she could begin to get over him and get on with her life.

'Go for it,' Robert said. He gave her a wink and a grin, then leaned across and bestowed a brotherly kiss on her cheek. Standing up again, he ruffled her hair, then sauntered across the compound to his own hut.

Courtney sat for a long time watching him go. Then her eyes turned towards the hut she shared with Aidan. In the darkness of the doorway he was standing there watching her. When their eyes met, he turned and walked back into the hut.

Moments later he came back out of the hut with a towel slung around his neck. Without looking her way, he strode down the path towards the river. Obviously he wasn't too worried about creating the impression that they were lovers tonight.

Courtney waited until he had been gone several minutes, then got to her feet and, carrying the mat she had been working on, moved towards their hut.

'Oh, there you are, darling,' her mother said. 'If you're looking for Aidan, he just went down towards the river.'

Courtney smiled. 'Thanks.' She turned towards her hut, and was stopped a second later by her mother saying,

'Aren't you going to go with him?'

'Not tonight. I'll wait for him here.'

Marguerite beamed at her. 'Wonderful idea. You can be prepared then.' She rubbed her hands together with such glee that Courtney wondered if even out here in the jungle her mother got magazine articles about being the total woman. Did she expect her daughter to stand at the door of the hut in a black négligé and nothing else, perhaps? Just waiting for her man to come home with a tapir for supper?

She didn't know, and she certainly wasn't going to ask. But she knew Robert was right—she and Aidan had to move on.

'Goodnight,' she said. 'Say goodnight to Daddy too.' And she went into the hut before her mother could comment further.

When Aidan came she was waiting for him fully dressed.

'I think we should leave tomorrow,' she said without preamble.

He blinked in the marginally brighter kerosene-lit hut. 'You do.' His voice was expressionless, acknowledging her words, not commenting on them or questioning them. She had no idea what he felt.

'Yes. I was talking to Robert and he said he thought . . . he thought . . .' she blushed as she got to this part '. . . honeymoons ought to be conducted in more privacy. And whether or not that's the case . . .'

'It is,' Aidan said flatly. He flung his damp towel on to the table and kicked off his shoes. The shirt he was wearing was hanging unbuttoned down his chest, and he began to do it up now as Courtney watched the movements of his fingers.

'Well, yes.' She jerked her eyes away from his chest, her mind away from the effect he had on her, and tried to remember reasons for leaving as soon as possible. 'That's what he meant. And although it really doesn't apply to us, of course, I'm sure you have plenty of things to get back to, and I know I do and...'

'You made your point,' Aidan said gruffly. He pulled a comb out of his duffel bag and bent slightly at the knees to bring his head in line with the blotchy mirror that hung on the wall opposite. He combed his hair, but his eyes connected with hers by way of reflection.

'So, shall we?'

'Whatever you want.' He scowled at his reflection, then at hers. Then he stood up straight, turned and stared at her, then raked his hand through the hair he had just combed, destroying all his effort. Her eyes widened in amusement. His narrowed in irritation.

He stalked across the room and put out the lamp, plunging them into the dark of the jungle night. Then he came over and lowered himself carefully into the hammock beside her. His body fitted against hers perfectly, the way it always did. She felt the tremble of desire surge in her again.

'It's probably a good idea,' he said almost into her ear. 'I don't think I can stand another night like this.'

CHAPTER TEN

LEAVING was easier—and harder—than Courtney had expected. Easier because Robert paved the way for her. Some time the next morning he got her parents aside and told them that it was time for her and Aidan to get a start on their own life together. Or words to that effect.

Whatever he said, it worked. For when Courtney merely mentioned the following afternoon that she and Aidan had to leave, her parents had apparently had enough time to rationalise letting her go.

'A husband must leave his father and mother and cleave unto his wife,' her father intoned, 'so I suppose the same applies to wives too.' He gathered her in his arms and gave her a hug. 'But we'll miss you, my dear.'

For the first time, Courtney believed that he actually would. His wedding sermon had impressed her, had made her proud of him, had taught her to see him in a new light. And she knew, as she hugged him in return, that in his way he loved her very much. 'I'll be back,' she promised.

'Of course you will,' her mother said. 'You won't even be that far away if Aidan is working in Boca Negra.'

'Oh well, we're not . . . not quite sure where we'll be,' she floundered. 'I have to go back to the States of course, to give the letter to Uncle Leander and the bank.'

'Ah yes, Leander,' her father muttered. 'Well, I can't say too much bad about the old devil. He did manage to send my daughter to me to get married, though it wasn't his intention.'

'No, it certainly wasn't,' Courtney agreed. She didn't want to speculate on what Leander would think of her marriage.

'But that's the way it is with the will of the Lord,' her father went on. 'He uses the strangest instruments to accomplish His will.' He ruffled her hair. 'Go, then. And God be with you, my dear.'

She gave her parents each one last hug. 'I'll see you soon,' she promised.

'Of course you will,' her mother agreed as they were shoving off. 'You'll be back for the baptism.'

'What baptism?' Aidan and Courtney asked together, looking around the tribe who had gathered to see them off. There didn't appear to be a pregnant woman in the lot.

'The baby's.' Marguerite gave an impatient shake of her head.

'What baby's?'

'Why, yours, of course.'

Courtney thought the silence must have stretched the length of the Amazon. Her eyes met Aidan's briefly, then flinched away again, not able to contemplate the pain she saw there. Reaching out, she gave her mother a last quick hug, forgiving her for a *faux pas* she would never know she had made. Then she sat down in the bow of the boat while Aidan pushed them away.

He yanked the starter, the engine sputtered to life, then, with a quick wave of his hand, he guided them out into the channel, around the bend, and into the jungle again.

They were alone.

And that was when it became harder to leave than she had thought.

For that was when she faced Aidan, her husband, without the artifice, without the sham, without the façades that had been necessary for the last week and a half.

And that was when she realised just how hard it would be to let him go.

She trailed her hand in the water, staring down into the murky depths, lost and aching.

'Get your hand out of there,' Aidan barked. 'You want to get it bitten off?'

She jerked her head around to see him glaring at her. 'What would bite it?' she demanded. 'You swim in the river.'

He scowled at her, muttered something about piranhas and alligators and other natural disasters. But she thought he couldn't be serious. After all, he did swim in the river, and she had never heard him comment or worry aloud about piranhas and such before. He was clearly just in a bad mood, and intent on taking it out on her.

But why? She would have thought he would be happy. Jumping for joy, in fact. The charade was over.

In case he'd forgotten, she said so.

'Yeah,' he agreed grimly. 'But we're still married.' He made it sound as if, even though the cell door had opened, the prison walls were still there.

'Well, rest assured, I won't hold you to it,' Courtney said sharply.

His green eyes narrowed. 'Nor I you,' he growled. His knuckles were white as he gripped the tiller.

'Good.' But she didn't mean it. And she was sorry he did.

The thought that she would have to leave him in a few short days nagged at her as time sped past. She supposed she should be grateful they were travelling upstream. Even with the engine doing the work, it took longer. And for all that he didn't seem inclined to talk or be friendly in the least, Aidan didn't appear to be hurrying.

He stopped frequently to swim, nothing more being said, she noted, about the dangers of being in the water. And when she mentioned it, he scowled at her.

'I'll be careful,' he said. 'Besides, I'm hot.'

'I am, too.' Which was nothing but the truth. And she was getting hotter by the hour, partly because of the increasingly humid day and partly because her desire for Aidan was increasing too. Maybe swimming was Aidan's answer to cold showers. She hadn't swum with him so far, at first preferring to keep a distance between them, then not wanting to provoke the passion that simmered beneath the surface after they were 'committed' to each other... especially after they were 'married'.

But now she changed her mind. Now, she discovered, she wanted to provoke. She wanted Aidan. And if she couldn't have him—well, maybe a swim would help a bit. And maybe—the guilty thought flitted across her mind before she could stop it—it would drive him over the edge of his control.

'I'm coming in, too,' she announced, and began to unbutton her shirt.

'You can't.' He seemed to strangle on the words, and he looked at her, horrified, as she finished unbuttoning it and tossed it into the bottom of the boat, then stood and undid the snap to her trousers. 'Courtney!'

'Why not?' she asked as the pants slithered over her hips. Aidan swallowed convulsively, unable to tear his eyes away. Then, without even noting whether he followed her, she slipped over the side of the boat into the cool river water. She ducked under for a moment, then surfaced, water streaming down her face as she turned to look up at him.

'Come on in,' she encouraged. 'The water's fine.'

He seemed about to refuse. A whole barrage of emotions warred on his face. But finally he shrugged and stripped quickly down to his underpants. This time he didn't take them off when, keeping his back to her, he dropped into the water on the opposite side of the boat.

When he surfaced he regarded her levelly over the bow which separated them. She looked back at him.

He is my husband. Immediately she tried to banish the thought. Only in name, she reminded herself. He didn't want to be. He was trapped, caught in a marriage no more of his choice than the first one he had made.

And it was up to her to see that he got out of it, no matter what she would have wished.

That meant no more smouldering on her part. No more aching desire. No more come-hither glances which, even though she meant them, could only bring disaster on them both. She needed to sublimate all her urges.

The thought made her smile. It was so like what her father would say. Well, in this case he was right. And there was no time like the present to get on with it.

'Race you across the river,' she challenged. And before he could reply, she had flattened out on the water and was churning towards the far shore, not waiting to see if he would follow.

He did. Almost effortlessly, he surged past her and was hauling himself up on to a log on the opposite shore while she was still several yards out. He watched her from beneath hooded lids as she stopped swimming, scrabbled for a toehold on the bottom, found one, and began to walk towards him.

All at once she felt horribly self-conscious, as if he could see every inch of her, inside and out. And as if he could read every thought in her head—most of them having to do with him, and none of which he would like a bit, she was certain. So much for all her sublimated urges. She stopped, tempted to turn and swim back to the boat.

'What's wrong?' He cocked his head, looking at her. 'Nothing.'

'Well, come on then. Or are you trying for a headstart in the other direction?'

She smiled brightly. 'It's a thought.'

'Can't wait to get back now, can you?' His voice was gruff.

She knew he meant to civilisation, not just the boat. 'Well...' Frankly, she could have waited a lifetime. But he wouldn't want to hear that.

She didn't have to perjure herself, though, because he stood up just then and said, 'I thought not,' then did a flat dive into the water almost next to her and began stroking back towards the boat. By the time she had swum back to it, he was already in and starting the engine.

So much for dawdling. If he hadn't been in a hurry, there was no question but that he was now. She clambered over the side of the boat, expecting him to stop and watch her, but he didn't even seem to notice.

They travelled until nearly dusk, scarcely speaking again. Then, when he saw what looked like a promising spot, Aidan steered the boat towards the riverbank and cut the engine. 'You wait here,' he told her. 'I'm going to check things out.'

'What things?' she called after him. But he had leapt lightly out of the boat and plunged off into the jungle without answering. She noted that he took his gun. While she waited she scanned the treetops apprehensively. But no jaguars were anywhere to be seen, thank heavens. Nevertheless, she was glad when he finally returned. 'What were you looking for?'

'Unfriendly inhabitants,' he said enigmatically.

'Jaguars?'

He shrugged. 'No. Outlaws, actually.' He was grabbing his duffel bag though, so she imagined he hadn't found any.

'Are there really outlaws hereabouts? As in ''stick 'em up, bang-bang, you're dead''?'

He gave her a wry smile. 'So I've heard.' He jerked his head towards the interior. 'Come on. I don't see any.'

'Why'd you think there were?'

'Something one of the Indians told me before we left. He said when he was out hunting he had seen a band of white men. Bad men, he described them. Big knives. Guns.' Aidan made a slashing movement with his finger across his throat. 'That sort of thing. He was pretty descriptive.'

Courtney made a face. 'Did he see them actually...?' She wasn't sure she wanted to know the answer even as she asked.

But Aidan shook his head. 'No. But while you might use knives like those to cut sugar cane and hack your way through the jungle, you don't use rifles that way.'

'But we have a rifle,' she argued.

'So we do. Maybe they're as harmless as we are, then,' he said blandly, tying his hammock to one of the trees with quick, economic movements. 'But I wouldn't bet on it.'

She didn't. In fact, for all that she tried to pooh-pooh his warnings, every scuffle in the brush, every monkey's leap among the trees, every creak and shriek made her jump. It was that, too, that kept her lying awake once they had eaten and Aidan had let the fire burn down to a dull orange glow.

It wasn't because she was missing the feel of Aidan next to her, the steady sound of his heart and the warm press of his hands on her back. It wasn't!

She flipped over in her own hammock, telling herself firmly that she ought to be glad she had a hammock to herself again. There was nothing worse than having to share one, than being crammed next to another person, having no space, no room to breathe. She sighed. *The lady doth protest too much, methinks,* she told herself wryly. A foot or so away Aidan shifted around irritably, then muttered something.

'Are you asleep?' she whispered.

'What do you think?' came the growl from the other hammock.

'Why not?'

He flipped over again so that he was facing her now, and he lifted himself up on to one elbow. The better to glower at her, she supposed, though she could scarcely see him in the dark. 'How the hell do I know? Mosquito bites, maybe.'

It wasn't the answer she had been hoping for. 'Do you really think so?'

He made a strangled sound.

'Would you like me to check? I could rub some calamine lotion on them and...'

'For heaven's sake! I'm all right! I just can't sleep, damn it. And your hands on me wouldn't help a bit, thank you very much! Now goodnight!'

'Goodnight.'

So much for the fond hope that he was missing her next to him the way she was missing him. So much for all her fond hopes, period.

It would be best, she knew, if they got back to Boca Negra as quickly as possible so that they would not be alone again. It was hard enough being around him in the daytime, wanting him, telling herself that she had a perfect legal right to him—he was her husband after all—and knowing she had no moral right at all. But another night like this one she wasn't going to be able to stand.

If Aidan had done something, said something, to change her mind, she would have been the happiest woman in the world. But he didn't.

Never much of a talker, he said less the next day than he had said in any of the preceding two weeks. He looked grim and morose, frowning every time she looked at him.

She understood. He still wanted her physically, and he was getting more frustrated by the minute because he couldn't have her. Not without jeopardising their chance of an annulment anyway.

Well, he wasn't any more frustrated than she was, that was certain.

The day was long and hot, and the tension grew between them like a storm about to break. The prospect of another night together hung over them like an angry cloud. There seemed no way to avert the disaster until, just as she was unloading the boat for the night, she spied three scruffy men in a canoe coming downstream.

One of them waved to her and shouted something.

Courtney paused as she was shouldering the duffel bag she had gone back for and looked at them curiously. The one steering had changed his course and the boat was now coming right towards her.

'*Bom día! Bom día!*' the one in front boomed at her, a grin splitting his swarthy, stubbled face. He said something else in Portuguese too rapidly for her to understand.

She shook her head. *'Sou americana.'*

Immediately the one who was handling the tiller spoke up. 'Texas, little lady. I'm from Texas.' He was burly and sunburned, with a battered straw hat clamped on curly, sandy hair. 'M'name's Deke, and this here's Sonny.'

Sonny was even more portly, obviously a man who enjoyed his beer and victuals. He looked as if he enjoyed many of the baser pleasures in life, and the grin he gave her made Courtney glad when Deke went on, jerking his head at the dark-haired man who had spoken first. 'That's José.' He pronounced it as if it were the girl's name, Josie. 'Fancy meetin' you out here.'

'Uh, yes.' Courtney smiled at them and began edging back into the bush where Aidan was hanging the hammocks.

'Settlin' in for the night, are you?' Deke went on as he used one of the oars to pole the canoe in towards the shore.

'Yes. My hus... husband and I are just...'

'Husband?' Deke looked at the other two men and shook his head. 'You got a husband? Now ain't that a shame? Pretty girl like you, married.'

'How 'bout we share a meal with you?' the one called Sonny said. He stood up in the canoe, his blubbery body making it pitch before he stepped ashore.

'Just a neighbourly meal?' Deke gave her an encouraging smile. 'We share our rations with you all, and you share with us.'

'Well, I...'

'We'd like the comp'ny.'

What was she supposed to say? No? And did she really think they would just blithely hop back into their canoe and head downstream if she did? Besides, she thought, ever ready to put the best complexion on the events at hand, if they stayed around, she and Aidan wouldn't have the privacy that was so wearing. There was no way

if these three were around that they could spend the
evening obsessed with what they *could* be doing, if
only...

'Yes,' she said with more firmness than she felt. 'Do
join us.' Turning, she led the way into the jungle.

'We have company,' she announced unnecessarily
when she found Aidan squatting before the fire he had
started, opening a can of beans for their dinner. At her
words he stood bolt upright and his eyes flickered—
where? Courtney's gaze followed his—to the *gun*?

She gave him an irritated look. They might be grimy
and a bit disreputable looking, but surely he didn't think
these men were the outlaws they had been warned about?

'This is my husband, Aidan,' she said to the men following her. 'These are Deke and Sonny and José.' She
gave the slight, dark-haired man's name its proper
Portuguese pronunciation, and he seemed to spare her
a flicker of approval.

He was the only one who did. Aidan was clearly furious. He stood, feet apart, hands loosely clenched, his
eyes darting around, sizing things up. Only when they
lit on Courtney did they linger, and the gaze he gave her
was so filled with anger, she was relieved when it moved
on.

'I thought we could share our meal with them,' she
began, trying to paper over the situation with words.
'Sort of a change of pace.' She tried to say with her eyes
what she thought they needed a change of pace from,
but Aidan didn't appear to notice. A muscle in his jaw
ticked.

'And we'll chip in a bit, too,' Deke offered. 'Sonny
caught some fish earlier.'

His words were met with stony silence.

'Isn't that nice?' Courtney said when it was clear
Aidan wasn't going to say anything.

'Terrific.' The one word came out through Aidan's
clenched teeth. He took a step towards the gun.

Courtney frowned at him.

Sonny frowned, too, also stepping forward. All of a sudden, and quite amazingly for a man so large, he jumped between Aidan and the rifle and whipped a long and vicious-looking knife out of his belt.

At the same instant José grabbed her, yanking her arms behind her back and pinning them there. She jerked, trying to pull away from him. But his hold was like a manacle, and she stopped struggling a second later when a smaller but no less deadly knife flashed in front of her face.

'For God's sake, you could have waited until we'd eaten,' Deke snapped at Sonny.

Sonny didn't even glance at him. 'An' get shot meantime?' He sidled over and picked up Aidan's rifle. 'No, thanks. Let's just get on with it.' He cradled the rifle against his forearm, the barrel pointing right at Aidan's chest.

Deke sighed, then shrugged. 'Well, all right, if that's the way you want it.' His gaze shifted to Courtney whom he regarded with a nonchalance belied by his next words. 'Your money or your life, sweetheart.'

'My——'

Aidan did step forward then. Sonny brought the end of the rifle barrel right up against his chest. 'Don't.'

Aidan stopped dead.

'We don't have any money,' Courtney tried.

'No?' Deke sounded disbelieving. 'Supposin' you show me.' He motioned for José to let her go, then waited while she opened her duffel bag with trembling fingers and tossed its contents on the ground. Deke pounced on her wallet, extracting the notes and stuffing them in his pockets. He scowled at the folded packet of traveller's checks, then riffled through her clothes, holding up a pair of bikini underpants, mortifying her and making Sonny lick his lips. Then he jerked his head at Aidan. 'Dump his gear, too,' he commanded her.

She looked at Aidan. The muscle in his jaw was ticking furiously, but he held himself under steely control. Only his eyes moved, and then his head in an almost imperceptible nod. Courtney crossed to the other side of the campfire where his bag lay and unzipped it. She took it, emptying it out, trying to scuff his wad of money out of sight under the leaves on the ground. But Deke saw her and jerked her foot, knocking her on her bottom at the same time as he snatched the wallet and opened it. His face was almost comical when he shook it and nothing more than three small notes fell out.

'That's it?'

'She told you, we don't have much money,' Aidan said flatly. 'Some people don't lie.'

'Some people don't live long enough,' Sonny said prodding him in the chest again with the rifle.

'Leave him alone,' cried Courtney, trying to scramble to her feet again.

'Rather we went after you, sweetheart?' Sonny gave her a leering grin.

'I'd rather you——' she began hotly when Aidan ground out,

'Courtney, shut up!' His green eyes glinted fire and she closed her mouth contenting herself with a glare at Deke, which promptly turned to outrage when he hauled her roughly to her feet.

'Let me go!'

'Not for a second, girlie. Let's see what else you got.' He spied the narrow gold chain she wore around her neck. 'That for instance. Take it off.' With trembling fingers she did. And then he saw the ring. 'That, too.'

'It's . . . it's my wedding ring,' she protested.

'Ain't that just too bad. Give it to me. Now!'

It shouldn't hurt so much to take it off. It was a ring her father had had, not one Aidan had picked out. It wasn't even an heirloom really. And it certainly wasn't a gift from a man who really wanted to be her husband. Yet parting with it hurt desperately. She swallowed hard as she tried to draw it off her finger. Aidan had put a thick wad of tape around it so that it wouldn't fall off, and it didn't remove easily.

'Hurry up!' Deke demanded, thrusting a grimy hand under her nose. 'We ain't got all night.'

'It's not worth that much,' she argued. 'Couldn't you just . . .'

'Lady.' The knife point touched her chin. 'The ring.'

She shuddered, swallowed, then twisted it, twisted it again, pulling all the time until at last the ring came free. Deke snatched it out of her hand and pocketed it without a second glance. She felt as if he had stolen her heart. Lifting her eyes, she looked at Aidan. His face was stony and unreadable. Whatever he felt, she was sure it wasn't close to what she felt. He couldn't imagine how badly she wanted that ring to remember their marriage by after he was gone.

'Come on.' Deke gripped her by the arm and began half dragging her back towards the boats. 'You're comin' with me.'

Out of the corner of her eye, Courtney saw Aidan start to move after them. Then Sonny cocked the rifle and said with quiet menace, 'I wouldn't if I was you.'

'Where are you taking me?' she demanded as Deke shoved her roughly down the path ahead of him.

'We're gonna check out the boat, you and me.'

'But——'

'No buts, girlie. You just do as you're told an' ain't nobody gonna get hurt.'

He gave her a shove and she stumbled through the trees towards the riverbank. She tried to look over her shoulder to catch a glimpse of Aidan, but Deke was between them, shouldering her on. She stopped at the water's edge.

'Now what?'

'Now you just get in that boat and toss the stuff out to me.' He indicated the two reed baskets that were still sitting in the bottom.

'You won't want them,' Courtney told him. 'They're not worth anything to you. Just odds and ends from the Indian tribe where we——'

'Lady, I don't want their history. I want them. Now toss 'em over.'

She looked at Deke, then at the knife he waved, and wondered why she had ever thought having him and his friends share dinner was a good idea. And as for making things less tense between Aidan and herself... there was a laugh. Grimacing, she got in the boat and lifted the first basket out.

All at once she heard a crashing noise in the woods. Deke, who had been watching her, jerked around, scowling back towards the way they had come. 'Sonny?' he yelled.

For a moment there was no reply, and Courtney felt a wild surge of fear mingled with hope. Had Aidan escaped? Then Sonny's voice drifted back to them. ''Sawright. No problem.'

Deke smiled, one of his coolly nonchalant smiles that Courtney could see now were cruel as well. 'Keep moving, sugar.' He gestured at the basket with the knife he held.

Hopes dashed, Courtney kept moving. She set the basket on the bank, then turned back for the other one. She didn't even see Aidan when he leapt out of the shadows and toppled Deke into the river.

'God!' Deke thrashed in the water, then sank, Aidan on his back, choking him.

Courtney scrambled out of the boat and tried to wade in to help him. Deke still had the knife. He twisted, trying to shake Aidan off, trying to slash him with the sharpened edge. But Courtney grabbed his wrist and twisted hard, wrenching it free.

The knife fell into the water, and with it went Deke's enthusiasm for battle. When Aidan flung him on to the bank and shouted at Courtney to get the rope out of the boat, he didn't even put up a fight.

'How did you——?' Courtney began, but Aidan shook his head.

'Get the engine going. Now.'

'Aidan, I——'

'Hurry up, unless you really want to stay and share a meal—and God knows what else with them.' His voice was mocking and bitter.

Courtney hurried. By the time he had Deke tied to his satisfaction and had groped through the outlaw's pockets for his own money and Courtney's, she had reloaded the baskets and had the engine going.

'Good,' he muttered, and, helping himself to the canoe paddles from the other boat, he jumped in. 'Move out,' he commanded.

The last thing Courtney saw of Deke he was rolling on the bank, hands and feet tied, shouting for Sonny and for help.

'How did you...' she started to ask again. But her heart was hammering so loudly and her hands were shaking so badly that she couldn't even get enough control to finish the sentence.

Aidan finished it for her. 'Get away? Sonny got a little careless. He thought he'd check through the food supplies, just to see if I'd hidden anything in them. He told me to move. I moved—to the other side of the fire. I kicked it in his face.'

She couldn't help wincing. 'And José?'

'He didn't have a gun. He wasn't hard to overpower when Sonny was out of commission.'

'That scuffling was you, then?'

'Yep.'

'But Sonny said he wasn't having any problems.'

Aidan gave her a grim smile. 'Amazing what a man will say with a knife at his throat.'

Courtney shuddered.

'Forget it,' Aidan said gruffly. 'It's over.'

But it wasn't easy to forget. The farther they went upstream in the darkness, the more likely it seemed to Courtney that Deke or Sonny or José might be lurking behind any tree. And whenever Aidan moved to tie the boat again for the night, she said, 'Do we have to?'

Finally he said, 'Yes, damn it, we do,' and proceeded to tie up at the next likely-looking spot. 'Come on.'

Courtney gritted her teeth and did what he told her, but she didn't like it. She didn't let him out of her sight, nor the gun either.

'They aren't anywhere close, for heaven's sake,' Aidan growled at her when she jumped a foot after a family of monkeys crashed through the tree branches overhead.

'Who knows what might be out there?' Courtney asked darkly.

'Not me,' Aidan said easily. 'But I'll bet you won't invite it home for dinner next time.'

'I didn't really *mean* to invite them. I just thought we'd have less . . . less . . . well, I thought . . .'

He looked at her narrowly. 'Yes? What did you think?'

'Nothing,' she muttered.

He caught her arm when she tried to pull away from him. 'What did you think, Courtney?'

'I thought things might be a little less tense if we had company,' she snapped, irritated.

His mouth twisted into a grin. 'Not quite.'

'No. But how was I supposed to know they were the outlaws?'

'With names like Deke and Sonny? What'd you think they were? Rhodes scholars on an anthropology expedition, for God's sake?'

'I don't judge people by their names,' she said stiffly.

'You don't judge people well at all.'

She just looked at him unable to even answer that.

He dropped her arm and raked his hands through his hair. 'Oh, hell, I'm sorry,' he muttered. 'Come on. We might still be able to catch a bit of sleep tonight.'

He had managed to bring along the hammocks, thank heavens. If he hadn't, they would have been forced to sleep in the boat. But he hadn't brought much else, not wanting to hang around Sonny and José while Deke still had her. Something else she owed him for, she thought glumly. Her honour, her happiness, and now, her life.

He rigged the hammocks in silence. Courtney helped where she could, but he seemed intent on doing it himself, and she thought, under the circumstances, the less she said at this point, the better. Finally he jerked the last rope and turned around.

'There. That should do you. All right?'

She nodded, then mumbled yes, afraid he couldn't see her bob her head in the darkness. She wanted to run to him, throw her arms around him, hug the life out of him and feel his strong arms around her, delirious with joy that he was safe and not lying dead of a knife wound back in the jungle somewhere. She said instead, 'Can I get you something to eat?'

She saw a grin glint in the moonlight. 'Dinner at last, you mean?'

She shuddered involuntarily.

'Never mind,' he said and gave her an awkward pat on the shoulder. 'I couldn't eat anyway. I'm bushed.' And with that he tipped back into his hammock. She heard it creak as his weight made it swing.

She couldn't eat anything either. Nor did she think she would be able to sleep. But she lay down anyway and stared up into the jungle canopy overhead. It was no different from last night, and it made Deke and Sonny and José seem like nothing more than a bad dream. But then she remembered the crawling fear, the glint of the knives, and she broke out in a cold sweat all over again.

At least they didn't kill us, she reminded herself. And Aidan even got the money back. Not that it mattered terribly.

But he didn't get the ring. She sighed, the fingers of her right hand moving to caress the bare ring finger on her left. She felt the slight indentation on the underside where the tape had pressed. Her throat grew tight and her eyes blurred, but she swallowed her tears.

'What's wrong?' Aidan's voice broke the stillness, letting her know she hadn't been as discreet as she had hoped.

She sniffled. 'Just thinking.'

'About...them?'

'Not them exactly.'

'They won't be back,' he promised.

'No. I wasn't worried about that.'

'What then?'

She sighed. 'I was...was thinking about...the ring.' She imagined he would tell her she was stupid, they were lucky to get away with their lives.

He didn't say a word.

'We were lucky to get away with our lives,' she said for him.

'Yeah.' His voice was low. She heard him shift uneasily in his hammock. She wanted to go to him desperately, wanted to hold him and have him hold her. But she couldn't. How could she ask him to do more than he had already done?

'I'm sorry,' she muttered.

'Me, too,' she thought he muttered. Then she heard the tree creak again, and all was quiet.

She woke some time past midnight. The barest sliver of moonlight enabled her only to pick out the closest trees and vines as she separated greys from blacks. She was surprised she had slept at all. But maybe their close call having been just that—close and nothing worse—had given her body a sense of relief that resolved itself in sheer exhaustion. In any case, she murmured yet another prayer of thanksgiving that they had come through their last scrape intact, then yawned, stretched and rolled over.

To discover she was alone.

She jerked to a sitting position and reached out a hand, groping for Aidan, disbelieving. But the faint white of his empty hammock was all there was. Her head whipped around, seeking him out.

'Aidan?' Her voice was rough with sleep and fear.

No answer came.

'Aidan?' Sharper now. Panic setting in.

She lurched out of the hammock, hitting the damp ground with a squish, then she scrambled towards the river, calling his name. Aidan didn't answer. And at the riverbank she discovered why.

The boat was gone, too.

'Aidan?' This time it was no more than a whisper, the breath gone right out of her. She was trembling so badly she had to grab a tree to keep from falling in, for there was no other conclusion to come to—Aidan had left her.

She slumped to the ground, shaking in disbelief, confused, frightened. Gone. How could he have gone? *Where* could he have gone? And why? The questions tumbled around in her head, each more baffling than the last. And for none could she find an answer. Finally she stumbled back to her hammock and crawled in. There was nothing else she could do until morning came at least.

And then?

Then she wasn't even sure.

She didn't sleep, just huddled there, trembling. Every wuffling in the brush, every scamper overhead magnified. And none of them Aidan.

The first grey light of dawn was just beginning to draw sharper distinctions between the trees and the sky when she heard footsteps.

It could be Deke. Or Sonny. It could be one of the Indians from the tribe they had first visited. It might even be the one she most wanted to avoid. She didn't care. Didn't even bother to feign sleep. She jerked upright and stared wide-eyed, heart pounding.

'Aidan!'

He stumbled into the tiny campsite, grabbing on to the tree at the foot of her hammock for support.

'What happened? What's wrong? Where were you?' The questions tumbled out. She fairly flew at him, rage and worry commingling.

He didn't speak, just held out his hand. When she held out hers to meet it, he dropped something into it.

'My ring.'

She didn't even have to see it. She could feel the warmth in the gold from the heat of his hand. The tape stuck to her palm. Her eyes flew to his face. 'You went after my ring?'

He shrugged. 'It was your father's.'

'To hell with my father,' she shouted, horrified at what he had risked. 'You could have been killed.'

He slumped heavily into the hammock she had just vacated. 'I wasn't.'

But he didn't look far from it. The grey light made his pallor terrible. Lack of sleep? Fear? She didn't know what it was. She only knew he was back. And she wanted to kill him at the same time as she wanted to rejoice.

'How could you? What did you do?'

'I went back.'

'They were still there?'

'Of course. You didn't think they'd go anywhere, did you? We took their paddles. Besides, it was getting dark when we split. And they certainly didn't think they were likely to be robbed.' He grinned almost painfully. 'I surprised them.'

'You terrified me.'

'Sorry. I thought you'd be glad.'

'If you got yourself killed?'

'You wouldn't have to worry about an annulment then.' He tried it as a joke, but she couldn't smile. The thought was too horrible.

'You must be exhausted.' She started to fuss over him then, babbling in her relief. And that was when she saw the dark seeping stain on his shirt.

'My God.'

'What?' He peered at her fuzzily.

'What happened?' She was tearing at the buttons of his shirt now, practically ripping them off.

He glanced down dispassionately, as if it were someone else bleeding like a stuck pig. 'Sonny got a little careless with his knife.'

'I thought you got his knife.' The wound was long and nasty, below his ribs and to one side.

'He took it back.'

She shuddered. 'You're an idiot to have taken the chance.'

'Thanks.'

'Well, really...' She was almost crying now. How could he have done something that stupid? And for a ring? Did he think she wanted the ring and not him?

'It'll be all right. I've just got to bind it.'

'It should be stitched.'

He gave her a baleful look. 'Do you sew?'

'If I have to.'

'Wait until it's light then,' was all he said. Then his eyes closed, and while she bound the wound as tightly as she could with one of his undershirts, he fell asleep.

They didn't have much *cachaça* left. But what they did have, she made him drink before she sewed his wound. He made a face while he drank it. At six in the morning, it wasn't the best tonic in the world. But she was glad they had something, for all the time she was sewing him up, she could feel his muscles clenching.

She did it while he was lying in the hammock and she was straddling him. She tried it first sitting to one side. But every time he flinched, the hammock swayed away. In the end, she lowered the other hammock and moved him over there, then clambered over him so that she straddled his thighs. With one of her feet firmly on the ground on either side of him, even if he flinched, he still couldn't sway away.

It worked. But when she was done and looked at his face, she was aghast to see it clenched and white from pain, sweat on his brow and a thin line of unshed tears under his lashes.

She wanted to cry too, wanted to comfort him, and when she said, 'Finished,' he breathed again and sighed, then reached for her and pulled her down against his chest.

She went willingly, wanting it—wanting him. 'Oh, Aidan, my God, how could you? It was only a ring.'

His arms tightened around her, hugging her fiercely, and her feet slipped off the ground as she pressed into him, warm and secure in his arms, exactly where she wanted to be. It was like coming home. She knew she had been missing the comfort of his closeness ever since they had left her parents, but only now did she realise how much. And how much she loved him.

He could have died. And for what? The tears which she had kept at bay all the time he was gone, the ones she had swallowed all the time she had been stitching him up, putting on a brave front so that she could get through it, poured down her cheeks now, dampening his neck and shoulders.

'Hey,' he murmured. 'Hey. It's all right. I'm OK. I'm fine.' But his hands trembled as they stroked her back. And after a long moment during which she could feel him straining for the control he had mastered so long, he suddenly let go and began to kiss her hair.

She returned the kisses, feathering them along the side of his neck, then along the line of his jaw. She lifted herself away from him to balance again on her toes, threading her fingers in the thick brown hair at his temples, smoothing the taut skin over his cheekbones with her thumbs. His own hands tugged the shirt-tails out of her trousers, then slipped underneath, callused fingers setting satiny skin on fire wherever they roamed.

'Oh, God,' he muttered. 'So soft. So sweet.' He fumbled with the buttons, then succeeded in releasing them, and eased the shirt off her. His hands came up to cup her breasts, freeing them from the scrap of lace that was her bra, and letting them spill softly into his hands.

She shivered, then burned. His touch was magical, sending the blood pounding through her veins, making them sing and throb as the aching need to be one with him exploded inside her.

Aidan's own need pressed against her, hot and hard where she straddled his body. And as his hands stroked her breasts, his hips lifted against her, speaking to her of his desire. She responded, bending to kiss him at the same time as her hands played down over his shoulders, then danced lightly through the hair on his chest, circling his nipples, making him shiver. She smiled, loving the way she could make him respond. Loving him.

His hands dropped from her breasts, going to the snap of her khaki trousers. The brush of the backs of his fingers against her stomach made her muscles quiver. He stopped.

Lifting his eyes to meet her, he asked for the world in one word. 'Courtney?'

She smiled and gave it to him. 'Yes.'

CHAPTER ELEVEN

COURTNEY discovered then that she wasn't her father's daughter for nothing. Just as he was willing to risk everything for what he believed in, so was she. And what she believed in was the power of love.

Whatever Aidan felt for her—and she couldn't pretend to know what that was—she loved him. And she needed to show him that love, needed to share it with him, needed to show with her actions the real commitment she felt to this man who was her husband.

And so she gave him her love.

She said 'Yes' again, then bent her head and pressed her lips against his, which opened hungrily for her questing tongue. He groaned softly, his fingers moving against her belly, working loose the fastener of her trousers and drawing down the zipper. Then his hands slid over her hips, pushing the khaki fabric down and off her legs which had come up alongside his in the hammock.

Her clothing dispensed of, he quickly set about removing his own. But she felt him wince as he bent forward to remove his own trousers, and she moved to help him. In seconds they were together again, naked now, their bodies trembling in need, aching for the closeness that had been denied them so long.

Aidan's fingers stroked her breasts, then caressed her ribs and smoothed across the soft skin of her abdomen, moving downwards towards the centre of her desire. One of his legs thrust between hers and his hand followed it, seeking her, finding her, and now it was her turn to moan softly as he stoked the fires that burned inside her.

'Please, Aidan!' She moved against him and felt him stiffen.

'I need you,' he muttered. 'I need you now!'

'Yes. Oh yes.' And she guided him home. Feeling at home herself, as if everything else she had seen and done in her life lost significance when measured against the rightness of what was happening this very moment.

She felt the urgent thrust of his hips against her and began to move with him, feeling the same need building deep within herself that she saw in the taut passion of Aidan's face. He twisted beneath her as she stroked down eagerly. The waves of climax broke over them, first Aidan and a split second later herself. Then she slumped against his chest, spent, depleted, exhausted, and whole at last.

Aidan's hand came up and brushed against her hair softly and slowly. Then he sighed and the stroking stopped. His hand lay limp against her back, and under her ear she could hear the gradual deceleration of his galloping heart.

She lifted her head off his sweat-slick shoulder and looked down at his face. His eyes were shut, the taut lines that so often furrowed his forehead and scored between his nose and mouth were softened. The passion gone, replaced by peace. He slept.

Courtney dropped her head and left a gentle kiss in the middle of his chest. Then she settled herself against him, careful that she wasn't touching the stitched and bandaged wound. Then she, too, slept.

She awoke less than an hour later to find herself hugged firmly against his side, her head resting on his shoulder, his breath teasing her hair. With extreme care she eased herself up and away from him.

She didn't wake him, though it was light enough now to travel. There was no rush. Not now. The only thing she had to get back for at all was to see that Uncle Leander and the bank got that letter from her father. And that could wait a few more hours at least. It could wait days if it had to. In fact, she realised with a smile, she could send it by post and not go back at all.

Edging out of the hammock without making it swing an undue amount, she knew that that was what she wanted most of all. She wanted to stay with Aidan. For ever.

And what did Aidan want?

Well, he wanted her. Or at least he had given a very good impression of it.

But did he want her enough to stay married to her?

That she didn't know.

She knew that life didn't come without risks, however. And she knew that she had just taken the biggest risk in her life. Compared to loving Aidan, being thrust ahead of everyone else when they entered a new village was nothing. Then she could have been killed, of course. But it would have been over in minutes. This way she could die slowly of a broken heart.

She wanted a lifetime with Aidan. She wanted love, children, a home, a future. And she didn't know if he felt the same way at all. He had got her back her ring, of course, she reminded herself, twisting it now on her finger, loving him for getting it at the same time as she hated him for having risked his life. But what did that mean?

She glanced over at him, still asleep in the hammock, his dark hair tousled, his lips well kissed, and wondered how he would look at her when he opened his eyes. That would be the key to their future.

That would be the sign.

Aidan blinked. His hand went at once to his side, touching the shirt she had torn up to make a bandage for his wound, patting it, then stopping abruptly. He blinked again, then turned his head slowly, looking around, remembering.

Courtney could almost pick out the instant he recalled exactly where he was and what had happened. It was when his hand had gone still against his ribs and reality had come rushing back.

She had been sitting by the fire, watching him, waiting for him to awaken. Looking forward to it, and yet dreading it at the same time. And now it had come. She smiled at him. It was a soft smile, a hesitant one. She would have liked to run to him and throw her arms around him. She would have liked to be that confident of his love.

But she wasn't. And she didn't. She only waited.

For a moment it seemed as if Aidan was waiting, too. They simply looked at one another, neither moving. Only weighing, assessing. And concluding. Concluding what?

That she didn't know. The sign she was looking for wasn't clear. It wasn't even there. Aidan looked pale again. His face, gentler and younger in repose, was unreadable now. It was as if he wore a mask to disguise what he felt. The only thing alive about it was the expression in his eyes. And they seemed intent on studying her. They never left her for an instant. And yet it wasn't love she saw in them. Nor passion. It was— God help her—worry, frustration, pain.

She shut her own eyes, hoping it would go away. She prayed she was wrong. And when she opened her eyes a moment later, she thought she might have been. There was no expression in his at all now. They were blank, non-committal. The eyes of a stranger.

'Hello, sleepyhead,' she said.

He grunted, shifted carefully, wincing when he put too much pressure on his side.

She got quickly to her feet. 'Let me help you up.'

He moved then, even more rapidly, and she could see him gritting his teeth. 'It's all right,' he said through them clenched. 'I can manage on my own.' And before she could get to him, he had stumbled to his feet and had gone off into the jungle by himself.

She knew better than to follow him there. But she hovered about anxiously, the words, 'Are you all right?' on the tip of her tongue, though she had the good sense not to ask them.

A few moments later he came back and reached for his trousers, tugging them on, studiously ignoring her. He tripped and almost fell, grimacing as he did so. Then finally he got them zipped up and reached for his shirt.

'I washed it,' she said quickly. 'It's drying down by the boat. There was...a lot of blood.'

In the clear light of day she had almost gagged to see the three-inch rip in the fabric and the splotches of blood that were almost dried down the length of one side of his shirt. But she had washed it out carefully, removing as much of the stain as she could. She would sew it when it was dry.

'Thanks,' he muttered, then grimaced again as he bent over and fished a similar shirt out of his duffel bag.

He had slipped it on his arms and was about to button it when her studied detachment ran out. 'Wait. Let me see your side.'

He glanced down at it, then proceeded to button the shirt. 'It's all right.'

'Aidan...'

'It's all right.' His voice was sharp, brooking no objection. He sounded like the man she had first seen on the dock, grimy, belligerent and hard-eyed. He looked the same way, too. There was nothing of the gentler man, nothing of the man who had said, 'I need you,' nothing of the lover she had known in the night.

He stepped away before she could get to him and began to untie the hammock ropes. 'We'd better get going.' He glanced pointedly at his watch, as if they were late for a train or something.

Courtney frowned. 'We don't have to rush, do we?'

He turned and gave her a hard look. 'I have a job to do. I can't just dawdle around in the jungle to suit you, you know.'

She stared, aghast. Then, 'I am paying you!' she snapped, stung.

His eyes narrowed and he turned and slammed his fist into the tree beside him, muttering something graphic and harsh under his breath. She shook her head, unable to equate this man with the one she had come to know. A sense of shame crept up on her. Had he thought she meant she was paying him for last night, too?

Oh, Lord. Mortified, she spun away and darted back through the jungle to the boat. She started rolling up the few pieces of wet laundry that she had done while he was sleeping, her movements all mechanical, her mind spinning out of control. When Aidan came up behind her a few minutes later, she was in no better shape, so she ignored him.

He did the same. Stowing the gear he had carried down along the sides of the boat, he went back for another load. So much for asking her to stay with him. So much for her spending the rest of her life as his wife in the jungle. She stashed the laundry in the mesh bag and went to help him pack.

It was a silent exercise. Aidan apparently had no inclination to speak, and Courtney had no idea what to say. What could you say to a man who was your husband for all the wrong reasons, with whom you had made love for all the right ones, and who now seemed to wish you would drop off the face of the earth?

Miss Manners didn't cover that.

Courtney did ask if he would like a bit of breakfast. There was a chance, she thought, that all this morose behaviour and snappishness might simply be due to an empty stomach.

'No,' Aidan growled.

And that was that.

On the surface at least. Inside the turmoil was still as great as ever. Courtney sat in the bow of the boat, feeling the scorch of Aidan's eyes on her back, and tried to figure things out.

Perhaps he was embarrassed and that was what was making him so short with her. Perhaps he hadn't expected that she was a virgin and now he didn't know what to say. Maybe her inexperience had disappointed him, angered him. Something had, that was certain.

She turned and glanced at his face, hoping to surprise some emotion there that would tell her what he was choosing not to say in words.

What she saw was anguish. And anger. He was looking right at her, and yet the moment she turned, his eyes slid away to contemplate the jungle they were passing and his expression grew hard and stark with something like pain.

Pain. And they were right back where they started—to the pain of the animal who knows he is trapped and can't do anything about it.

She felt her throat tighten, and swallowed hard, blinking against the tears that sprang unbidden to her eyes. In her mind she could hear her father intoning, ''Tis better to have loved and lost than never to have loved at all.'

But she was hard pressed to believe it at the moment. She wondered if she would ever come to believe it at all. She wanted to ask Aidan what was wrong, but wasn't sure she wanted to hear the answer. Maybe if she waited. Maybe if she walked carefully, quietly. Maybe everything would even out.

Aidan, frankly, didn't seem to care. All he seemed intent on was getting back upriver as quickly as possible. Courtney wondered briefly if it was because he thought Deke and Sonny might come after them. She even ventured to ask him. But the response she got was merely a disbelieving snort. Whatever Aidan was worried about, it wasn't another encounter with the trio of outlaws.

The Indians were a different matter. Courtney had forgotten about them until they were almost on top of the place where she and Aidan had run into the hunting party on the voyage down river. But, when she saw that particular narrow strip of beach, remember she did, and she wished for once that Aidan would make the boat go faster.

She was astonished to find him turning it in towards the shore and cutting the engine altogether.

'What are you doing?' she demanded, swivelling around to glare at him.

'Stopping for the night.' He was scowling at her from beneath the hat he wore and he looked no more pleasant than he had earlier in the day.

'Here?'

'Here.'

'But why? I mean, considering the circumstances under which we left . . .'

'I doubt anyone knows about those, except your "friend",' he said scathingly. 'And I want Santos to look at my side.'

'It is bothering you.' She pursed her lips and glared at him, annoyed that he had spent the whole day in pain without telling her so.

'It's all right,' he said just as he had that morning. But she didn't believe him any more. She just scrambled out of the boat, then waited for him to get out and tie it up before they headed inland towards the village.

She didn't see any of the Indians until they were almost on top of the group of huts. But the Indians had seen them and were waiting for them. The chief rushed to meet them, all smiles and broken Portuguese greetings. Obviously Aidan was right. Her amorous friend had not broadcast his failure to bed her.

Thank heavens. But this time she wasn't going to take any chances. Besides, this time she *was* Aidan's wife.

That he hadn't thought of that just proved, she decided, how much pain he was really in. For when the chief embraced him, he withstood it stoically, then asked if Santos, the medicine man, would take a look at him.

'*Sim, sim.*' The chief nodded vigorously. 'You hurt. You show Santos. He make you better. Come.' And he motioned to the man called Santos and began to lead Aidan towards the hut he had occupied last time. Courtney picked up her duffel bag and followed.

By the time she entered the hut Santos had Aidan lying on the hammock, stripped of his shirt, while he probed the wound, scowling and muttering as he did so.

Courtney watched nervously, knowing that her stitching wasn't the best in the world, then wondering if an Amazonian medicine man could have done it better.

'Not bad,' Santos decreed at last. 'I make poultice for it. That help you a lot,' he said to Aidan, then turned to nod briefly at Courtney. 'You do a good job,' he acknowledged.

Aidan's head jerked up as he noticed her for the first time. 'What are you doing here?'

'I belong here,' she said flatly, unwilling to let him shut her out now.

'You say he not your man,' the chief reminded her.

'He wasn't,' Courtney agreed. 'He is now. He's my husband now.'

'Husband?' The chief positively beamed. 'Oh, yes?' He rubbed his hands together gleefully and looked to Aidan for confirmation.

Aidan glowered at her.

'. . . for richer, for poorer, in sickness and in health,' Courtney reminded him.

He sank back into the hammock, unable to fight her any more.

'You smart girl,' the chief complimented her. 'You get your man.'

Courtney gave him a wan smile and wished it were the truth.

Santos, meanwhile, bustled around taking small bags of herbs and mixing them with water, then heating them together and stirring them, blending them into a pungent-smelling poultice that he finally carried over and placed gently against the knife wound below Aidan's ribs. Then he beckoned to Courtney.

'You wrap this on,' he told her in halting Portuguese, his hands moving to show her what his words failed to convey. 'Then you sit with him. You watch. Later you take more——' he indicated the mess still simmering in the pot over the fire '—and do again, yes?'

'Yes,' Courtney said promptly.

'Hey, why can't you do it?' Aidan protested, lifting himself on his elbows as best he could, scowling at Santos who was shaking his head.

'Too mean, me. You want wife.' Santos smiled benignly. 'Is what wives good for.' He nodded again at the pot bubbling away, gave Aidan a smile of encouragement, Courtney a wink, and walked out.

'Damn!' Aidan slumped back against the hammock, his jaw working, his eyes glinting anger.

'Be still,' Courtney said. She put her duffel bag on the floor of the hut, then went out and got his and brought it in as well. Aidan watched her irritably, but he didn't comment until she had set them side by side and was kneeling down riffling through hers.

Then he said gruffly, 'You don't need to bother with me.'

'No bother.' And without giving him a chance to reply, she gathered up her things and headed for the door. 'I'll be back. I'm going to freshen up a bit.'

When she came back half an hour later he was, as she had hoped, asleep. He lay on his back in the hammock, his shirt off, the bandage snug against the wound, one hand trailing alongside the hammock, the other over his eyes.

He looked altogether dear and familiar. Asleep, of course, he would, she thought wryly. But just let him open his mouth! But he wasn't opening his mouth now. He was snoring gently, the hard line of his mouth softened now, the implacable stares smothered by his arm.

She tiptoed around, putting her things away, trying not to wake him, knowing full well how badly he needed his sleep. Last night he wouldn't have had any. And he had worked hard today getting them this far upriver. The sooner to get rid of her, apparently. The thought made her sigh, and she set about hanging the second hammock with a heavy heart.

Then she carefully changed his poultice, fearful of waking him. But he was sleeping soundly and he scarcely moved when she took off the pack that Santos had put on and replaced it with a fresh batch. The wound seen to, she bent her head and brushed a kiss across his lips.

'I love you.' She whispered the words she wouldn't dare tax him with if he had been awake.

The sound of him muttering woke her about midnight. 'Are you all right?' she asked him softly.

'Wh——? Where——?' He tried to sit up, then fell back against the hammock, groaning.

She rolled out of hers. 'What is it? Shall I get Santos?'

'Santos?' The one word seemed to reorientate him. 'I remember now.' He eased his body around gingerly, then growled, 'What are you doing here?'

'Staying with you.'

'It isn't necessary.'

'Santos said——'

'I don't care what Santos said. I don't need you!'

'Then I need you,' she told him flatly.

'What?'

'Surely you haven't forgotten my local "friend"?'

He paused. 'Oh, yeah.' Then, rolling on to his side, he sighed as if resigned to a terrible fate.

Courtney felt an almost overwhelming temptation to kick him. The man who had loved her so well last night had vanished into thin air. This one was the one who had flipped her into the water the first time she had met him.

'Don't worry,' she said to him starchily, 'I won't ravish you again.'

His head snapped around, and she could feel him glowering at her even in the darkness. 'What's that supposed to mean?'

'I should think it was clear.'

'As mud.'

'Well, you certainly don't seem happy about what happened between us last night.'

'Forget last night.'

She cringed. So much for the declaration of love she had fervently hoped for. Obviously it was the furthest thing from his mind. He wanted out. Desperately. Not even a night's loving had changed his mind.

In fact, she realised with horror, it had simply compounded his trap.

'We can't get an annulment now,' she said dully, the realisation stunning her.

'No,' he said so grimly that she knew he had already thought of that. 'We can't.' He turned his head away from her, staring into the blackness beyond. 'But we can get a divorce.'

Her parents should have named her Pollyanna, she thought miserably one week later. Because even despite Aidan's pronouncement, she held out hopes.

Even after they got back to Consuelo's and he carried her bags in and left her with the briefest and most perfunctory of farewells, even after he didn't come around to enquire about her for the rest of the week, even after she almost ran into him in the marketplace and, seeing her coming, he ducked behind a produce stall and escaped out the other way, she still thought he might come around. She couldn't get the night they had spent in each other's arms, the loving and the needing that had passed between them, out of her mind. And she hoped he couldn't, either.

But obviously Aidan thought more about what a trap she had got him into.

Well, it was her own fault for expecting anything else. Aidan had never lied to her. He had never told her that he was getting engaged to her or marrying her for anything more than the expedient reason that he did.

But it didn't stop her feeling miserable every minute of the day.

'You don't look so good,' Aurelio told her that morning when she was listlessly packing her clothes.

'Mmm.' She didn't feel so good.

'You get a fever in the jungle, maybe?'

'Maybe.'

He lounged on her bed, leaning against the wall, regarding her with the solemn curiosity of a true student of human nature. 'I think maybe it's catching.'

Courtney frowned at him. 'What do you mean?'

'I think Aidan got it, too.'

'Aidan doesn't look so good?' She felt a momentary heartening at the news. She hadn't seen Aidan close enough to tell since he had left her at Consuelo's seven days ago.

'Looks very bad,' Aurelio said promptly. 'All hollow under the eyes. All the time angry, too.'

So what else is new? Courtney wanted to ask. But she just folded another shirt and placed it carefully into her duffel bag. 'I'm sorry to hear that.' She dropped the last piece of freshly laundered clothing into the bag and zipped it shut. 'There. That's that, then.'

Aurelio sat up. 'You ready to go.'

She sighed and stared out of the window down towards the river, thinking about what might have been, about what would never be now. 'I'm ready,' she said.

'I go check on the bus.' Aurelio launched himself off the bed and vanished down the hallway to see if anyone had heard how close the bus was to Boca Negra.

When she had got back last week, she heard right away that it wouldn't be through for several days. Three or four at least, Consuelo apologised. Courtney hadn't minded. Not at first. She had thought that having to stay around for a few days she might discover that Aidan had changed his mind.

But as the days passed and he did everything he could to avoid her, she had to revise her thinking.

He wasn't going to change. Nothing was going to change. And then she started thinking that the sooner the bus arrived, the better.

This morning Aurelio had come in and reported that word had come through that it was on its way. Word of mouth, even through the jungle, seemed to move faster than the bus. All day long she had waited. She had packed, then unpacked. Then packed again. She had

walked the length of the hallway fifty times. She had
walked to the marketplace twenty times at least. She had
even, once, walked down towards the river. But when
she got close enough to see that Aidan's boat was still
there, she had turned and walked quickly back to
Consuelo's. However much she might want to see him,
it would hurt too much to have to say goodbye to him
again.

So she was totally unprepared for the knock on her
door that was immediately followed not by Aurelio's en-
trance, but by Aidan's.

She stared, her heart and mind hungry for him,
drinking in the sight of him. He did look 'not so good',
just as Aurelio had said. His features were gaunt and
sleepless—hunted, she thought. Or, more accurately,
trapped. His green eyes were dark, like the depths of the
well she had once seen in Yucatan, and just as fathom-
less. His mouth was pressed into a firm line, but it looked
more weary than hard now. And he looked more resigned than angry. She wanted to go to him, to touch
him, to smooth the cares away from his brow, to soothe
his hurts, and comfort his pains. But she was the cause
of them all, so she stayed where she was.

'You're leaving now.' It wasn't a question.

She nodded, unable to speak yet, still not quite able
to believe in his presence here, wondering what it meant.
She looked from him to the duffel bag. 'Aurelio says
the bus is coming this afternoon.'

'That's what I heard.'

They looked at each other, their eyes probing, asking
questions neither would voice. And the answers? They
weren't forthcoming either. Finally Aidan said, 'I'll carry
your bag for you.'

'Can you? Is your wound healing?'

'It's fine.' He strode into the room and picked it up,
then turned on his heel and went back out, leaving
Courtney to stare after him. She remembered doing it
before, watching him walk through the jungle, her eyes
feasting on the easy grace of his loose-limbed walk, the

confident set of his shoulders, the proud tilt of his head. If she closed her eyes she could imagine him in a courtroom, striding back and forth cross-examining a witness. But that fantasy just brought her face to face with reality—the reality of his first marriage, the reality of the life he had left, had sworn he wanted no part of again. The reality that the only thing he wanted out of any marriage was divorce.

She took one last look around the small, shabby but spotless room and knew she would never forget it. Then she followed Aidan out of the door.

Behind the desk, Consuelo looked up with interest when Aidan and Courtney came down the hall. She had been looking at them with interest ever since they had got back last week. But though she dropped enough veiled queries about what had happened between them on the trip, which Courtney could never bring herself to answer, at least she never asked outright. Now she just clicked her tongue and shook her head. Aidan scowled at her and walked out of the door without comment. But Courtney couldn't leave like that.

She went over to say goodbye and was enveloped in a warm, sisterly embrace.

'I'm sorry you go,' Consuelo said, wiping a tear from her eye. 'You so good for him.' Her eyes flickered to Aidan who was standing on the porch, his back to them, his hands on his hips as he squinted up the road for signs of the bus.

Courtney's gaze followed Consuelo's. 'I would like to have been, anyway.'

'Maybe he see sense, run after you, marry you.' Consuelo, too, seemed to want to look on the bright side. It was a good thing she didn't know Courtney and Aidan were already married. It would have destroyed her outlook on life.

'A happy ending?' Courtney said ruefully.

'Like a book,' agreed Consuelo, smiling.

Flying footsteps resounded just then, and Courtney heard Aurelio shouting, 'It's coming! Raimundo says

the bus is coming.' He shot past Aidan and in through
the screen door, letting it bang behind him. 'It's coming,'
he told Courtney again, as if she hadn't heard the first
time.

'Thanks.' She gave him a hug, too. Then she
shouldered her bag and went out on to the porch.
Aurelio started to follow her, but his mother held him
back.

Aidan turned as she came up behind him, his
expression dark and unreadable.

'Raimundo says the bus is coming,' Courtney told him.

'Good old Raimundo.'

'Yes.' She wondered what would have happened if he
had been the one to take her to find her parents. Would
she be married to him now? A look at Aidan—at the
quick glimmer of emotion in his eyes that vanished
almost as abruptly as it did in hers—let her know his
thoughts had gone along the same lines.

Then she heard a shout from the road, 'Here it comes,'
and the cloud of dust that surrounded the bus came into
view.

Their gazes met again.

Tell me you love me and I won't go, she said to him
with her eyes, with her heart.

Silent, Aidan looked at the ground.

The bus ground to a halt in the dirt road right
alongside the hotel. The door opened and an Indian
woman with a chicken, and two scruffy looking men,
got out. The driver looked at Courtney and Aidan
enquiringly.

'Coming?' he asked.

'She is.' Aidan climbed the steps and slung the duffel
bag into the seat the Indian woman had just vacated,
stood for a moment surveying the rest of the passengers,
then dropped lightly to the ground and came to stand
in front of her.

She looked up into his face, trying to memorise it.
Unsure she wanted to, the way he looked. His expression
was grim, taut, like steel. Hard and ungiving. But in her

heart she could only see another Aidan, the tender one who loved her, who caressed and cherished her, who willingly married her because she had needed that. She wanted to tell him that she appreciated it, to tell him she would never forget him. But she knew that words of memories and tenderness were just what he didn't want.

She twisted the ring on her finger, the ring he had almost died for. And she knew she couldn't speak. Even if keeping silent nearly killed her.

She touched his face. One last fleeting caress of a sandpapery cheek. She swallowed hard. 'Goodbye, Aidan.'

He held her gaze.

The bus driver tapped his fingers on the steering-wheel. 'Are you coming or aren't you?'

Courtney didn't hear. Her mind belonged to Aidan. He bent his head swiftly and touched his lips to hers.

'Get the divorce, Courtney.'

And before she got on the bus, he was gone.

CHAPTER TWELVE

LEANDER PERKINS'S face fell at the sight of her.

Good, Courtney thought, because outfoxing her uncle was about the only satisfaction she was going to know.

'You didn't go?' Leander took one look at her pale, sad face and sounded hopeful as he stared up at her from behind his wide walnut desk. His plump fingers tapped on the blotter. They clenched a second later when she nodded and said,

'Oh yes, I went.' She pulled the letter her father had written out of her bag.

Leander scowled, then reached for it. She gave it up, unsurprised when he didn't even unfold it before slipping out his lighter and burning it to ashes. Then he smiled at her, the benevolent uncle. 'You'll have to do better than that, my dear.'

Courtney smiled back, knowing him all too well. 'I did,' she assured him. 'That was only a copy. The original is in the hands of Mr Thurston at the bank.'

The colour drained out of Leander's face. 'But you—you can't! I need—I have——! You have no right! No right at all!' he blustered, coming to his feet like a walrus emerging from the sea. 'I need that money, miss.'

'My parents need it, too,' she told him firmly.

'Your father is a wasteful, foolish man.'

She didn't deny it. A saint would be a wasteful, foolish man to Uncle Leander, and there was no doubt her father had little monetary sense. Which was all the more reason he needed his inheritance, but she couldn't expect to convince Leander of that. 'You have your fair share, uncle,' she said calmly.

'I need it all!' Leander stamped in a small circle behind his desk, then halted and fixed her with his beady little eyes. Punching a buzzer, he summoned his secretary. 'See Miss Perkins out,' he commanded. 'You'll regret this, missy. You'll regret you ever went down there. Just wait and see if you don't.'

Courtney didn't have to wait, she already knew. It had been nearly a month since she had come back, and every day felt like a hundred years. Every night she spent dreaming of Aidan, torturing herself with 'if onlys' and 'might have beens'. And none of it did any good. She was as miserable now as she had been when the bus rattled down the road and Boca Negra vanished round the bend.

That was why she had bothered to come and deliver the bad news to Uncle Leander in person. It was the one sweet success she was going to have in the mess that had become her life. It might be gloating—it *was* gloating— but heaven knew, she needed something to feel good about. There wasn't anything else.

She let Uncle Leander's secretary see her to the door without protest. His threat was idle and she knew it. They both knew it. For the time being at least, Uncle Leander was stymied. Next year, of course, her father would have to indicate that he was alive and well again. But next year was his problem. There was no way she was going back to the jungle after him again.

Ordinarily a trip to Wilshire Boulevard would have occasioned some window-shopping and perhaps a nice meal. But Courtney didn't feel like it today. She had no enthusiasm for anything. So she drove back to Manhattan Beach, put her car away, then dragged herself up the steps to her apartment in the frozen state of mind she had been in since she had got home.

She had a deadline on a book. But she looked at the thin manuscript with a total lack of interest. She had bills to pay, but she couldn't make herself sit down and get to them. She had letters to answer. But no letter had come from the man who mattered most in all the world.

Not, of course, that she had been expecting one. If Aidan had written, she would have died of surprise. Just as well, then, she thought wryly as she took out a can of soup for supper, that he hadn't.

She dumped the soup into a pot, then stood by the stove and waited for it to heat. Her mangy tomcat, Fred, wove between her feet, meowing, demanding attention. She fed him, then carried her soup to the table, poured it into a bowl and sat down to eat.

She wasn't hungry, hadn't been since she had come home. She had lost weight, hadn't slept, and in general wasn't the woman she used to be. It was what came, she thought, of expecting happy endings. When you didn't get them, you went to pieces.

'Like Humpty Dumpty, I am,' she muttered into her soup bowl. The realisation wasn't cheering.

One thing she knew for certain, she wasn't going to be able to give Aidan the divorce he wanted. Not right away at least.

The day after she had got home, she had dutifully opened the Yellow Pages to look for a lawyer, but the tears swam in front of her eyes, and she hadn't been able to think, much less write down any names and addresses. So she had put it off.

The next week she had tried again. That time she had got as far as writing down a name and had even driven by his office. But she couldn't make herself go in.

She *didn't* want a divorce. She wanted Aidan. And if she couldn't have him, he couldn't have his divorce right this minute either. She wasn't ready yet to give up her fantasies. Besides, what difference would it make? He wouldn't even know. Who was going to tell him, out there in the middle of the Amazon jungle, for heaven's sake?

So she had shut the phone book again, telling herself that she would take care of it when she felt more at peace with herself. Some day, she told herself, she would be over him. She would be ready to date again, to meet men again, to get involved. Some day she would meet a man who would make her forget.

But it was going to be a long time, she knew that.

She confirmed that half an hour later when, while she was washing up, the doorbell rang. It was Clarke.

'You've been avoiding me,' he accused her, brushing past her into the living-room and flopping on to the sofa.

That wasn't precisely true, but she certainly hadn't rung him up when she returned either. She couldn't see any point. Now she merely shrugged and offered him a cup of coffee.

'Why didn't you call me when you got back?'

He obviously wasn't going to leave it alone. 'I didn't have anything to say.'

Clarke scowled. He surveyed her critically while she put water in the pot and set it on to heat. 'You're too thin,' he told her. 'Starving yourself?'

'No. Just not especially hungry.'

He sat up straighter. 'Some jungle bug. I told you so.'

'It isn't a bug.'

'What is it, then?'

Aidan, she thought. 'Just off my food, I guess.'

'I knew that trip wouldn't do you any good. Said so, didn't I?'

'Yes, you did,' she replied quietly, setting out the cups and saucers. She remembered that Clarke took milk and wondered if Aidan did. They had never drunk coffee together.

'And I was right,' he informed her importantly.

She didn't agree or disagree. From her parents' standpoint, of course, he couldn't have been more wrong. From her own? Well, she was miserable. He had certainly been right about that.

'So come sit down and tell me what's new.' He patted the couch beside him. But she didn't take him up on it. She waited until the coffee had perked, then she poured out the cups and added milk to his. Then she carried him one and took her own half-way across the room where she sat on a wing-back chair all by herself. Clarke looked annoyed, but didn't comment other than to repeat, 'What's new?'

She was tempted to tell him she was married. That was news. And it would have got rid of him post-haste, and that would have been nice. But she couldn't hide behind Aidan. She had done that enough in the jungle. Here at least she had to learn to stand on her own two feet.

So she simply told him about her trip, maximising the travelogue aspects, and minimising any references to the travel guide.

Clarke listened with not very much interest. The moment she stopped, he said, 'Well, I hope you've got it out of your system.'

'Yes.'

In fact nothing was further from the truth. Sometimes she thought she would die for wanting Aidan. Fred leaped on to her lap and curled up, kneading her thighs with his sharp claws.

'Good.' Clarke nodded as if she had come to her senses at last. 'So how about going with me to the music centre tomorrow night?'

'No, thank you.'

He looked at her surprised. 'You have another date?'

She hadn't been dating anyone else when she had left, and she wasn't a fast enough worker that he could imagine she could have met someone new since she had come back. He would die if he knew she had married a man she had known scarcely two weeks. 'I'm busy,' she said, volunteering nothing else.

He scowled. 'Playing hard to get. I won't wait around forever, you know, Courtney.'

'You shouldn't,' she agreed wholeheartedly. 'You can do much better than me.'

That did take him aback. He had expected her to be contrite and to welcome him with open arms. 'Are you brushing me off?'

'Letting you down gently.'

'Don't bother!' Clarke sprang to his feet and carried the coffee-cup over to the counter. Banging it down, he turned to glare at her. 'I'm not a charity case, no matter what you think.'

Before she could reply, he stalked out of the apartment.

She watched him vanish down the stairs, feeling guilty, tempted to go after him. She knew she should have handled it better, but she didn't know how. She was at a loss as to how to do anything these days. Her ability at interpersonal relations seemed virtually nonexistent. She really hadn't wanted to alienate Clarke. Heaven knew some day she might be ready for his attentions.

No, that wasn't true. She wasn't ever going to be ready for him. She was, she was beginning to fear, a one-man woman, just the way her mother was. And the man was Aidan Sawyer.

She couldn't even deny that, for a split second when the doorbell had rung, she had felt a searing hope that when she opened the door Aidan would be standing there.

He hadn't been, of course. Never would be. And her heart and her mind and her soul would just have to start getting used to it.

She told herself that again the next day when she was in the library doing some research and found herself consulting *Who's Who in America* to see if Ethan Sawyer was listed. But she couldn't put the book down when she discovered that he was.

She carried it over to a table, where she had research books on Indian folk tales spread out, and sat down, entranced with this thumbnail sketch of one aspect of Aidan's life.

His parents lived in Brookline. His father still practised law, and his brother, Eamon, was a partner. There was a younger one, Dillon, and a sister, Mary Margaret. She found herself wondering about his siblings—if they were like him. She would have liked to meet them. But there was no chance of that. Nor would she ever meet their children. Aidan was an uncle, too, she discovered. His father had four grandchildren.

She lifted her head and stared straight out across the library, yet saw none of it. Her inner eye was imagining Aidan as an uncle, holding a child, remembering times she had seen him playing with the Indian children. Then it went further, picturing him as a father. He could have been a father if Shanna hadn't ended her pregnancy. Not for the first time did she wish he had fathered a child with her. Her eyes blurred over and she bent her head, shutting the book decisively.

Wishing was pointless. A dose of reality was what she needed now. She had broken things off irretrievably with Clarke. She had given him his walking papers so that he could get on with his life. She had to do the same for herself.

She put *Who's Who* back on the shelves and made herself get the phone book again. Then she copied down the address of the lawyer that a friend had recommended. It was time to stop dallying around. If not for Aidan's sake, then for her own, she had to get the divorce.

She almost didn't answer the doorbell when it rang again that evening.

The least innocuous person it could be was an encyclopaedia salesman or an Avon lady. More likely though, and worse by far, it might be Clarke, returning to the fray. He'd always been persistent, but she had hoped this time he would give up on her for good.

Presumably he hadn't, though, for the bell sounded again, loud and insistent, demanding a response.

Sighing, Courtney dried her hands on the tea towel and went to answer it, forming words of rejection as she went.

'I don't——' she began even as she jerked open the door, because it was a start she could use on anyone '—believe it.'

Aidan Sawyer stood on her porch.

Her words brought a frown to his face, then a rueful grimace that gave his mouth the faintest quirk at the corner. 'I'm not surprised,' he said. His voice was soft, hesitant almost, so unlike him that she was tempted to reach out and touch him to be sure he was real.

She still wasn't convinced of it. But he looked substantial enough as he lounged against her porch railing wearing a pair of freshly laundered jeans and an open-necked blue sports shirt. He was as darkly tanned as she remembered, but away from the overpowering greens of the jungle his eyes took on an even more startling hue. She looked at him for a long moment, and he looked back at her unflinching until she was the one who turned away, flustered.

What was he doing here?

He rubbed a hand round the back of his shirt collar, kneading the taut muscles in his neck. 'I don't suppose you'd invite me in, would you?'

Her lack of manners appalled her. 'Of...of course. I'm sorry, I——' But she couldn't offer any rational excuse. She was quite simply stunned. And Aidan seemed to realise it. His mouth curved a bit more, but he didn't look confident when she stepped aside to let him in.

She reached out and trailed her fingers lightly against his shirt sleeve when he passed, just to assure herself he was really there.

He was. And so was the bouquet of flowers she hadn't noticed because they had been behind his back. Now he thrust them into her hands and raked his own through his hair.

She stared at the daisies, nonplussed.

'They're for you,' Aidan said gruffly. He thrust his hands into the pockets of his jeans and rocked back on his heels.

'Er, thank you.' She waited for an explanation, but none was forthcoming.

Aidan was staring around her apartment curiously, glancing back at her every few seconds as if he were trying to understand it in relationship to her and vice versa. When he showed no sign of explaining his presence, Courtney shrugged and went to find a vase for the flowers.

She tried not to let herself speculate. But it was almost impossible. Aidan? Here? Her heart was doing a polka in her chest. She stuffed the daisies into an empty wine decanter and set them on top of the table beneath the bay window. Aware of Aidan watching her, she fussed with them for a moment, straightening this stem, then that one. But too soon she ran out of ways to keep occupied and had to turn to face Aidan and what he wanted with her.

He cleared his throat. 'You ruined everything, you know,' he said bitterly, leaning one hip against her kitchen counter.

She stared at him. 'I what?'

'That jungle used to be the best place there ever was.'

She found herself reaching for the table-top, gripping it tightly, her knuckles turning white.

'It had everything I ever wanted after I left Boston. Action. Adventure. Challenge. A new frontier. A new beginning.' His voice was rough, betraying a tension that seemed to vibrate throughout the room. He stopped and stared hard at her. 'I thought I was whole.'

A gaggle of skateboarders hooted past in the street. Courtney swallowed, not daring to say a word.

He bent his head and stared at the rug between his feet. 'Then you showed up.'

The words were barely a whisper, yet she heard them echo as if they had been hauled up from the depths of his soul. One look at him suggested they had been. He was looking at her now with an anguish such as she had never seen. The expression on his face made her take a step towards him, made her want to reach out and comfort him. And yet she didn't dare.

Because she didn't know yet what he meant. It sounded awful. But she wasn't sure. Had he come half-way across the hemisphere to demand an apology?

She waited still, looking at him half in hope, half in trepidation. And at her silence he seemed to become more and more agitated.

'I didn't want it, God knows,' he growled at last, scowling now, pacing the length of her apartment's tiny sitting-room. 'I never wanted it again.'

She tilted her head to one side, watching him pace, trying to keep up with his progress and his words at the same time. For a man who had never failed to make himself clear in the past, he was winning an obscurity award tonight.

'Aidan,' she said at last, her voice stopping him as if he had been lassoed and jerked to a halt. 'What are you talking about?'

He glared at her. 'You,' he snarled. 'Me. What the hell did you think I was talking about?'

'I wasn't sure,' she said honestly. She glanced at the bouquet on the table again. 'Aidan, why did you bring me the flowers?'

His scowl grew, if possible, even fiercer. 'It's customary, isn't it?' he demanded with bad grace. 'When you go courting you bring the girl flowers, don't you? Or chocolates. And I remembered what you said about the daisies.'

Courtney, stuck on the word *courting*, shook her head in disbelief. 'Daisies?'

'You said you'd have liked them for your wedding. So I thought...' He didn't finish the sentence. She finished it in her mind. Her heart somersaulted. She couldn't take everything in.

'Courting?' she asked, just to be sure.

A dark flush suffused Aidan's face, visible even despite his dark tan. 'That's what I said.'

'But——'

'I know what you're thinking,' he blurted. 'You got trapped into the marriage. I don't blame you for not wanting it. I got trapped once myself. But damn it, Courtney, I love you!'

'You...' She was about to repeat his words, astonished and disbelieving, but Aidan didn't give her the chance.

He crossed the room and grabbed her by the arms, hauling her against him, her face only inches from his own. 'I know I don't have any right to court you. I know I'm probably the last person on earth you want. And I don't blame you, but——'

She didn't let him finish. Instead she erased those few inches and placed her mouth over his, kissing him for all she was worth. She felt a split second's resistance, then he groaned and kissed her in return. His tongue invaded the warmth of her mouth, his body grew taut and hard against hers, his arms crushed her against his chest. Then, all at once, he thrust her away and said raggedly,

'I promised myself I wouldn't do that.'

She shook her head, perplexed and bereft.

'I came courting,' he said, 'not seducing. Not ravishing.' He sounded as if he were trying to convince himself as well as her.

'Why not?'

'Why *not*?' He virtually yelped the words.

'If you love me,' she began reasonably, her hand going out to stroke his arm which jerked under her touch.

'I'd be trapping you,' he said miserably. 'Our whole marriage was a trap.'

'For you,' she agreed softly.

'Not me,' he corrected irritably. 'You.'

'You think *I* was trapped?' The notion astounded her.

'I forced your hand. I told your father we were engaged.'

'But only because I needed to be engaged to someone.'

'No.'

'No?' She looked up at him curiously. A dull red flush had spread across his cheekbones and he shifted uncomfortably, running a hand through his hair, then shrugging his shoulders and staring at the floor.

'Ah, hell,' he muttered. 'I was in love with you clear back then.'

Her eyes widened. 'You were?'

'Damn it, you sound like a bloody parrot.'

'Sorry.' But she wasn't. She was smiling all over her face.

'But it wasn't right, what I did,' he went on doggedly. 'I shouldn't have trapped you that way. I should have tried to make you love me first, not married you. But I couldn't. I didn't realise...' He shook his head and she saw flickering pain in his eyes. 'So I had to let you go.'

He jerked away from her, striding to the far side of the room, rubbing his hand against the knotted muscles of his neck. 'I tried to, damn it. And I know I don't have any right to ask it, but...would you...would you let me...court you...now...? The right way?'

She smiled. 'Courtship is a preliminary to marriage,' she reminded him softly.

'I know that,' he growled. 'I'm all done being Peter Pan.'

She crossed the room and went up on tiptoes, brushing her lips across his. 'I'm delighted to hear it. There's just one problem.'

'What's that?' He scowled fiercely.

'You can't really court me when we're already married.'

'You've applied for a divorce,' Aidan said sharply.

'No.'

The world seemed to tilt on its axis. Their eyes locked. And Courtney saw her own flare of hope reflected in Aidan's beautiful eyes.

Then, as if he dared not let himself hope too much, 'I thought...I mean, I told you...'

She shook her head slowly from side to side. 'I didn't do it.'

'You...didn't...''

'I never contacted a lawyer.'

'But...' He was as reluctant to face his dreams as she had been. 'But...why?'

'Because I was selfish. I loved you too much to let you go.'

He simply stared at her. His hands, which clutched her arms, were almost bruising in their sudden strength. And when he finally found his voice it was raw and aching. 'You love me?'

He still didn't believe it, she could tell, and so she said it again. 'I love you. You are irascible and obnoxious, stubborn and opinionated, and I love you so much that when you let me go I thought I'd die.'

A laugh that was closer to a sob shuddered through him. 'You *do* love me?'

'Yes.'

And this time it was Aidan who was kissing her. Strong and intense, his urgency almost overpowered her. Finally, knowing that if they didn't move soon they would scandalise Fred, she drew him into her small, dimly lit bedroom where she pulled him down on to the bed.

It was different from the hammock, but no less wonderful. More wonderful actually, for this time she was sure of their love, and it was the farthest thing from a trap she could imagine. It was the most freeing, the most liberating feeling she had ever known. And when at last they lay damp and spent in each other's arms, she had the chance to tell him so.

'It seems like a dream come true,' he muttered, still clearly feeling as if he had taken advantage, when he just as clearly, to her, had not.

'You're going to have to start believing in happy endings,' she teased him.

He raised himself on one elbow and looked down at her, one of his hands smoothing over the curve of her hip. 'I'll try. But it isn't always going to be easy.' He shut his eyes briefly. 'Marriage scares me. I mean, I want it with you. And you *say* you want it with me, but . . . the situation is . . . just like what happened with Shanna. I forced you.'

'No one forced me.' She laid the palm of her hand against his cheek, stroking the rough stubble of day-old beard. 'I wanted it, too.'

He smiled then, beginning to be convinced. His green eyes sparkled. 'So long as you're sure.'

'Absolutely. Are you?'

'Oh, yes.' He grinned ruefully. 'My life as one of the Lost Boys is over. The river was my freedom for a time. I needed it. But I don't need it now. I need you.'

He kissed her again, tenderly this time. The urgency was past, but not the pleasure. Now their lovemaking was relaxed, gentle, secure in the knowledge that they had all the time in the world.

'When did you know?' she asked curiously much later when they lay wrapped in each other's arms again. She wondered why she hadn't seen it before when it was so clear in the light of his eyes now.

He gave a wry grimace. 'I don't know exactly. It sort of crept up on me. It probably started when you flipped me into the water.'

She laughed. 'Am I marrying a masochist?'

'No. Just a man who's impressed as hell with a woman who can give as good as she gets.' His hand moved seductively over her body.

'Oh, I can do that, all right.' And her hand moved to find him, stroking him, making him forget what he was about to say. He luxuriated in the tender caresses she gave him until he could stand it no longer. Then he drew her on top of him and framed her face with his hands.

'But I think it came home to me,' he said softly, 'when I listened to your father's wedding sermon.'

Courtney blinked. 'How so?'

'All those things he talked about. Honouring, esteeming, cherishing. I felt those things about you. And when he talked about the joys of marriage—about the fidelity, the constancy, the sharing...well, I wanted them, too. But I couldn't believe you wanted them. Not with me. That's why I wouldn't make love to you. It wasn't because I didn't want to, believe me.'

'But you did finally,' she reminded him.

'We might have died out there! I couldn't resist you when I thought of an eternity without you.'

'Good.' Then she frowned. 'But you were so remote afterwards. I thought you were angry.'

'I was. At myself. I'd taken you when I had no right. And I had destroyed your chances of getting an annulment.'

'Which I didn't even want.' She kissed his nose.

'Well, I didn't know that. You didn't say.'

'Because I thought I was trapping you.'

He laughed. 'What an altruistic pair we are, giving each other such freedom.'

She giggled and hugged him. 'I'd say we were a couple of prize chumps. And we almost blew it.'

'Yeah,' he agreed soberly. 'But we didn't. And that's what counts. I don't want a divorce, Courtney. I want you now and for ever. In my arms. In my life.' He searched her eyes for a similar commitment, a faint smile touching his mouth when he found it. 'Do you think we can manage all that stuff your father was talking about?'

'Love? Commitment? Fidelity? That sort of thing?' she asked him, smiling into his eyes.

'And a grandchild or two.'

She touched his lips with her own, sealing their fate. 'I wouldn't mind working on it,' she said. 'But it might take a while.'

He scowled. 'How long?'

'Oh,' she said, wrapping her arms around him and drawing him into the warmth of her life and her love, 'maybe another fifty or sixty years or so.'

AND THEN HE KISSED HER...

This is the title of our new venture — an audio tape designed to help you become a successful Mills & Boon author!

In the past, those of you who asked us for advice on how to write for Mills & Boon have been supplied with brief printed guidelines. Our new tape expands on these and, by carefully chosen examples, shows you how to make your story come alive. And we think you'll enjoy listening to it.

You can still get the printed guidelines by writing to our Editorial Department. But, if you would like to have the tape, please send a cheque or postal order for £4.95 (which includes VAT and postage) to:

VAT REG. No. 232 4334 96

- -

AND THEN HE KISSED HER...
To: Mills & Boon Reader Service, FREEPOST, P.O. Box 236, Croydon, Surrey CR9 9EL.

Please send me _____ copies of the audio tape. I enclose a cheque/postal order*, crossed and made payable to Mills & Boon Reader Service, for the sum of £_____ . *Please delete whichever is not applicable.

Signature _____

Name (BLOCK LETTERS) _____

Address _____

_____ Post Code _____